Hew
Against
the Grain

Betty Sue Cummings

Hew
Against
the Grain

Atheneum · *1978* · *New York*

TO *Hattie Jane Bruce Cummings*
and Kathleen McLaughlin O'Mara

Library of Congress Cataloging in Publication Data

Cummings, Betty Sue.
Hew against the grain.

SUMMARY: A young girl whose home is on the
Virginia-West Virginia border loses her will to live
after she becomes a victim of
the cruelties of civil war.
[1. United States—History—Civil War, 1861-1865—
Fiction]   I. Title.
PZ7.C9145He   [Fic]   76-25593
ISBN 0–689–30551–6

Published simultaneously in Canada by
McClelland & Stewart, Ltd.
Manufactured in the United States of America by
The Book Press, Brattleboro, Vermont
Designed by Mary M. Ahern
First Printing January 1977
Second Printing January 1978

Hew
Against
the Grain

One

Mattilda Repass loved Wabash Camp Meetings. This year she was determined to get religion, simply *had* to, since she was the only one in the family not yet saved. Today, the last day of camp, was her last chance.

She sat near the front in the huge Tabernacle shed with her family. Luella Patrick's family and the other slaves sat in the same row, blacks together, whites together, Mattilda and Docia Patrick the link between the races. Both girls listened fervently; both sought a call from the Lord. Time and past to get converted.

"And JEEsus," the preacher suddenly shouted into a pool of quiet, "JEEsus wants us to LOVE one another. Oh it's love, oh it's love, oh it's LOVE the Christian gets when he gets converted."

It was so true. Her whole family was loved and loving, Mattilda thought, and she needed to be like that too. But she felt no closer to the Lord.

She yawned, began to wonder what was happening out in camp. Nothing was going to happen inside yet. Nighttime was a better time to get converted anyway; she had observed this every year. So why sit here when there were explorations into new territory outside the shed? The excitement was all outside. Maybe she would make some new friends. Maybe meet some *boys*. Out in the campground they were apt to hear abusive voices sputtering over the coming election. Sometimes *women* wrangled over Bell, Breckinridge, Douglas, Lincoln. Once Mattilda had heard a husband scold his wife, "Hush now. You ain't got a vote." And she had replied with cool cheek, "Have y'all passed a law against our thinking too?"

Even games were different. Last year ironweeds were Roman spears; this year they were guns. Last year peejibs were poor children's marbles; this year they were clay bullets propelled by former marble players. (*Peejib* used to be a baby name. Now a *bullet*.) Last year getting saved was the chief concern; this year you got saved in the shed, but you argued outside.

You argued about the election, about cotton states Democrats, about slavery, about whose arsenals those federal forts *were* anyway.

You argued about WAR.

Mattilda thought about the war that might come, thought about the excitement outside of the shed. Tonight for sure she'd get religion. She elbowed Docia. "You need to go to the toilet?" Quick nod. They whispered to their mothers, who sighed and exchanged glances of resignation and agreement.

On the way out, Mattilda received a pat and a nickel from her oldest sister Sarah, who sat in proud happiness with her new husband, Jason. The gift of a nickel said, It's all right. You're young only once.

They were almost past the last big posts when the preacher's voice raised to a new level of excitement.

4

"Now I'll tell you *why* you need Jesus. Election's coming, my friends. Election's coming, and some of you will vote for the wrong man if you don't pray about it."

A dreadful silence filled the shed. The preacher had moved out of his proper sphere. Mattilda, greatly excited, stopped to listen.

Heedless of the unrest, the preacher charged ahead, "Some of you will vote for Abraham Lincoln, yes, you'll do it without prayer." His voice went to a shrill whisper. "Knowing in your heart, you're pushing us into WAR."

An agitated movement spread among the people, and near Mattilda a glowering man and woman stood up and stalked out, his boots thudding, her skirts swishing. Mattilda looked at her parents, Bland Senior and Dorothy Repass, who sat quietly, their faces pale with rage.

The preacher suddenly became aware of the turmoil. People jumped up, sporadic as popcorn, were settled by the restraining hands of their neighbors.

"Peace, my friends," the preacher said in a loud voice, his face red, puffy, *un*peaceful. Slowly the people settled.

Mattilda plucked at Docia's sleeve, and they went out into the sunshine.

The fresh air came at them in a light swoosh, and they breathed deeply. Docia did a quick freedom shuffle, and they ran to the women's section of woods where they stood guard for each other. Next to spend the nickel. Mattilda settled for a piece of chess pie, disappointingly like that she ate at home, and Docia chose a salty pickle. They ate as they wandered through the city of tents, multi-colored, variously shaped, placed helter-skelter. A wagon trail curved its way through.

People worked at drying out their shelters and airing the quilts, pitched horseshoes, played the fiddle, traded. Screamed at each other about the election. "Mr. Lincoln gets elected and

I'm moving to South C'lina, you watch," a man hollered. "Who's going to miss you?" roared the answer.

Mattilda shrugged, not clear about it. They went to the spring, Mattilda swinging a gourd dipper.

A boy about her own size lay on his stomach to drink directly from the spring. She grinned as he nudged an obstinate salamander away.

"Here," said Mattilda, offering him the dipper. He looked up. The intensity of his blue eyes shocked her. It reminded her of Grandpa Hume's self-description: "I'm a blue-eyed Scot." Whenever anybody tried to pin Grandpa Hume down on politics or slavery or religion or anything he didn't want to discuss, he would say, "Don't ask me, I'm just a blue-eyed Scot," which was *supposed* to mean he knew his place and wouldn't get beyond his depth in knowledge, but which indicated to Mattilda that the questioner didn't know enough to tempt Grandpa Hume into an argument. To *her* a blue-eyed Scot was a person of intelligence, courage, and restraint.

The boy accepted the dipper, dipped and offered it to her and Docia in turn, then drank.

"Are you a blue-eyed Scot?" Mattilda asked hopefully.

His intense stare became confused. "I'm Daniel Durham. You're Bill's little sister, aren't you?"

"Little! About as big as *you* are."

His head went down. She laughed to herself at his great hands and feet. Mama always said big hands and feet on a young'un meant a tall old'un. If he grew up to those feet, she'd not be tall enough to look him in the eye.

"Yes, I guess I am a blue-eyed Scot," he said finally. "Is that bad?"

"No, because my Grandpa Hume is one, and he's the best man I know."

He smiled, relieved. "Are you saved yet?"

6

"No. Docia ain't either."

Docia lifted her shoulders with a troubled shrug. "It's not because I don't try."

"Yeah. Me too," he said.

"The last night's the best to get converted, don't forget," Mattilda encouraged them.

There was a sudden rustle of leaves on the other side of the spring, and a man's voice grated, "What's a white girl doing here at the spring with boys and niggers?"

Lumping them and multiplying them and covering them with evil.

Mattilda's heart leaped out of place, and Daniel's face paled. Silently, with unspoken compact, the three got up and returned to camp, leaving the man glowering at them.

"Who in the world was that?" Mattilda asked, feeling dirty, feeling ashamed of something she must have done and couldn't recollect.

Daniel shrugged.

"That's old Ray Beard," Docia said bitterly. "You don't remember old Ray Beard? Your daddy sold oats and rye to him last year."

"Oh, yes."

They were silent, depressed. When they came to the wagon trail, they separated. "I hope you get converted," Mattilda said.

"Thank you," Daniel said. "You all, too."

"If that old Ray Beard got religion, I don't want my share," Docia volunteered.

All three laughed, and it wiped away some of the bad feeling, but the echo of his voice recurred in Mattilda's mind like a threat.

At night there were three preachers, one a Baptist, by invitation to accommodate the great numbers of Baptists who couldn't stay away. Excitement ran like lightning through the shed, and every preaching and every hymn built it higher.

"Oh hah," roared the Baptist. "Oh hah, I got to make a run tonight, Lord, help me make a run and save these sinners."

"Amen. Amen," agreed the congregation.

"Help me to open their eyes, Lord. Let them see Jesus. Let them feel his mercy. Let them know eternal grace. Oh, brothers and sisters, I want to make a run tonight."

"Amen. Amen."

A clapping started, a mild little spattering noise, and up front an old lady danced into the aisle, eyes closed, face turned with rapture toward the ceiling.

"Thank you, Lord," she screamed. She clapped and shouted.

"She's a Baptist," Mattilda's mother explained quietly.

"Oh," said Mattilda.

But then nearby, Mrs. Neal, neighbor and member of their own church, sprang to her feet, clapping and cheering, "Glory! Glory! Glory!"

Mattilda looked up at her mother. "There are Methodists and *Methodists,*" her mother said. We are not that kind then, Mattilda thought, and she regretted it because Mrs. Neal looked so happy.

"Oh, I can't make a run tonight," the preacher groaned and he bowed in sorrow. It was all right with Mattilda if he *didn't* make a long preachy run of language to encourage the unsaved to come forward. That never worked for her.

As if he had received her thought, the preacher stood bolt upright and looked with great passion toward the ceiling. He suddenly began to sing. "Amazing grace! how sweet the sound that saved a wretch like *me!*"

The congregation got caught up in it, and the song rang out.

Oh, it would be her undoing. Mattilda loved the lilt of the

song and the persistent booming beat as feet stomped the dirt.

There were more shouts and a move of sinners to be saved started forward. Oh, the song's power came at her. "I *once* was lost but now am found, was blind but *now* I see."

Her family sang heartily and the thumping rhythm pursued her. Oh, she did want that grace and power, whatever it was.

She saw Daniel Durham on his way to the altar. Oh, she must hurry before the meeting was over. A sudden movement beside her told her that Docia had made it and was on her way forward.

"Thank you, sweet Jesus," Luella cried out.

The power of the Lord had risen from the song and taken over the crowd. Only Mattilda had not yet found grace.

She sent up a wispy plea.

"Lord, I want to be saved and don't know how."

It was all she needed. She felt so relaxed and relieved at being in communication with God that tears filled her eyes and her heart hastened its beat. She stood up. This must be it, she thought; I'm converted at last.

Her family all hugged her as she went past this time, and she hurried forward, went down on her knees by Docia, the only black at the altar.

She suddenly saw Ray Beard again, glaring at her and Docia from the side of the shed. Never mind. Her family was there. Her father could face him down. The preachers were there. She had achieved amazing grace, and with God on her side, how could Ray Beard harm her? Not even the War could touch her now.

Two

Mattilda swam with her brothers and sisters in the murky mill pond. Suddenly she saw Docia at the edge of the pond, her face dark and wistful.

"Come on in, Docia," she called.

Docia wouldn't answer. Too shy of the older whites, Mattilda knew.

Mattilda, bidding for the admiration of her brothers and sisters, hollered, "Afraid that black will wash off?"

Docia yelled back, "Yes, and I'd hate mighty bad to turn into a sajer."

Mattilda's sisters and brothers grinned, and she felt outdone and snappish.

What in the world was a *sajer?*

Sarah's hand settled on her shoulder light as a bird.

"You reckon she'll apologize to you? Talking back to you like that?"

Mattilda hadn't considered that. "Her apologize to *me?*"

"Well, or you to her?" It was a question, not quite a suggestion.

If Sarah thought it was all right, it must be the thing to do. She nodded, waded through the muddy water to the bank, and up the path toward Docia's house.

Three

March 1861

Dorothy Repass hoped that the last frost had hit, so she put Mattilda and Docia to work cleaning the flower garden. Never mind that WE will freeze out here, Mattilda thought. Neither girl was sure which plants were flowers and which were weeds, so they indolently decided to let them all live. Pretty soon they got into a fight.

Docia started it.

"How you going like it when they name this place over again?" she asked, daring Mattilda with a slanted look.

"What you talking about?" Mattilda asked, seeing at once that Docia was in a smart-aleck mood and determined not to let it get her mad.

"New Place, Kanawha, United States, that's what," Docia said in triumph. "I'm surprised you don't know that. You know, white and all, can read and all, *know* everything and all. Surprised you found out something you don't know."

She is not going to get me mad, Mattilda told herself, her temper sharpening nevertheless.

"Kanawha? What in the world is that?" she asked, careful to appear indifferent, but sure from Docia's manner it was something of great importance. "Besides a river, I mean," she added.

"Ha!" Docia chortled. "I said you didn't know it! Well, miss, this state of Virginia is fixing to split into right-thinking people and wrong-thinking people. The right-thinking ones going live in Kanawha, and the wrong-thinkers will stay in Virginia.'' Docia's face was as bright as polished copper and her eyes shone with pleasure at the prospect.

Mattilda had no earthly idea what Docia was talking about. However ignorant she appeared, she must find out.

"Where will *we* be then?'' she asked.

"Probably be in hell,'' Docia said, brittle as a splinter. "That's the Virginia side. But *I'm* going to be in heaven. That's the Kanawha side.'' She smiled a white false smile at Mattilda. And, as always happened, Mattilda's temper flew away first. Docia had invited it.

"Nigger, nigger, black as tar,'' Mattilda said softly, "can't get to heaven on a railroad car.''

Docia always held her temper. She furnished the spark that set Mattilda off and got her to talking ugly; then she complained to Mattilda's mother and got Mattilda a good scolding, once even a spanking. It was hard to defend herself against Docia who was so quick, bright, angry, with a tongue like a flicking knife. Docia made her feel clumsy and slow.

But this time, she suddenly knew, she had *got* to Docia. Docia's face sulled up and turned away. Mattilda decided to push a little.

"Nigger, nigger, black as tar,'' she said again, experimentally, eyeing Docia.

Docia clapped her arms into a tight rejecting fold. She stared past Mattilda and interrupted delicately,

"Sajer, sajer, green as grass . . .''

"Can't get to heaven on a railroad car,'' Mattilda said loudly.

"Sajer, sajer, kiss my ass,'' Docia said, her broody eyes aslant.

"DOCIA! That's terrible!''

Mattilda gave Docia a good shove, no more than she deserved. To her utter shock, Docia shoved back. She smacked; Docia smacked. She kicked; Docia kicked. They grabbed each other, punched, fell, pulled hair, cried, rolled, yelled their obscene little rhymes over and over again to each other. They whirled and slapped. Mattilda's heart thudded and sweat poured down her neck, and pebbles hurt her back when she rolled, and her eye throbbed, and her nose bled, dripping with salt taste into her mouth. She was demoralized by what was happening, but fury would not let her quit.

At last both were exhausted, and they fell apart. They examined their wounds and torn clothes, their bodies heaving for air. Their anger was spent.

"Now look what you done," Docia said without anger. "My knee's bleeding all over my dress. Mama will beat me for this."

"So what?" said Mattilda. "Look at my bloody nose."

Docia looked. Her mouth dropped open.

"Oh, my Lord, they going *kill* me," she said. "I blacked your eye too. It's turning puffy."

She was so terrified, Mattilda felt she had to comfort her. "Well, that's no worse than I did to you. Look at all the cuts and scrapes."

Docia's face was agonized. "You don't understand *nothing*. Black child never hits white child—rule one. Black child never talks back—rule two. They going *kill* me, you'll see."

Mattilda puzzled over it. "Docia, you're just being silly. It's my fault as much as yours."

"Matt, for once in your life, understand something right. I MUST obey. I MUST give in. I MUST be polite. Now *you* don't need all those musts the way I do. It would be NICE if you obeyed and NICE if you gave in." Tears made Docia's eyes glisten. "I be scared all the time. You know?"

13

Mattilda suddenly saw. For the first time she realized the necessity for Docia, who was naturally lively as a cricket, to be mute and submissive, and she understood Docia's terrible unvented rage at having to be this way.

"I don't want it to be like this, Docia," Mattilda said sorrowfully. "But what can I do about it? Nothing. But Papa and Mama ain't going to beat you. Never."

"They never have," Docia admitted. "But a slave never knows. It hangs over my head. They might even sell me away from Mama and Lucas. You know?"

"We ought to get you free," Mattilda said. "Then you wouldn't need to worry."

"Kanawha going to do just that, Matt. They going to war over freeing us."

The *War* again! Mattilda tried to think about it but she couldn't. If there were a war, and they became Kanawha instead of Virginia, where would she belong? Would she be on Docia's side? It seemed like what she ought to do. Or on her parents' side? She *couldn't* leave her parents. It was a terrible problem, too hard to get the answer to.

"Well, I'll tell you what to do about *our* problem. Let's say we climbed a tree and fell out." Docia was enchanted with the lie. It might work.

"Docia, you care if I touch your hair again? It didn't feel right, not the way I expected it to."

Docia lifted an indifferent shoulder and leaned her head closer.

Mattilda crumpled a handful of hair and marvelled.

"How do it feel?" asked Docia, amused.

"Soft. I thought it would be more like little springs. Or wire."

Docia giggled. "No. No more'n yours is slick, the way I used to think."

14

They told their story together. Mattilda's mother studied them with a speculative smile, but she didn't question their story. She sent them together to Mattilda's room with pitchers of hot water so they could clean up. Wounded and giggling, they went upstairs.

Beneath her laughter, Mattilda felt uneasy. She had never fought Docia before. She felt as if the ugly old War she kept hearing about had reached out and tapped her with a heavy finger.

Four

The cordial grin on Ray Beard's face argued with his cold eyes and didn't fool Mattilda or anyone else in the schoolhouse. Facing Sarah, he held himself in a courteous half-bow.

"You know, Miss Sarah, it's against the law teaching them to read and all. It only stirs up trouble, or I'd never say a WORD about it."

Sarah, calm and unafraid, her back like a yardstick, stayed on her feet, even after Marjorie went white as a ghost and sat down.

Somebody ought to go for their father, Bland Senior, Mattilda thought. But not me.

As if he read her mind, her brother Bill suddenly got up and left. Sarah and Mr. Beard flicked their eyes at him but pretended his leaving had no bearing on the matter.

Lucas began making furious purpose noises, coughing and groaning, yawning loudly, finally dropping his slate.

You see? Mr. Beard's eyes asked in triumph.

"Lucas," Sarah said without turning. Lucas subsided. You see? her eyes mocked.

"I want to know your personal interest in this school," Sarah said. "You needed to interrupt our classes to express something important to you. Something personal. And I want to know what *is* this important thing."

Ah, good. What business is it of *yours?* she was saying. And putting it so nice. Not saying this is our building and you're standing here on our sufferance.

"Why, I'm just saying, Miss Sarah, that here you have two niggers and you're teaching school to them, and it's not right in the sight of the law, and it's my duty to report it if it don't quit. But it's also my duty as a friend . . ." Here he stopped to give his false bow again. ". . . my duty to warn you first."

Her father would be along soon to settle things. He'd settle Mr. Beard's britches for him.

Mr. Beard thrust his chin forward as if he'd completed the conversation. Mattilda hated it when he did that. Always jutting his chin out like he was pushing away a bad taste.

"But your personal reason?" Sarah persisted coolly, as if she were helping a pupil through a difficult problem. "We know you don't have a child here who'd be harmed by Lucas or Docia."

"Got a cousin!" he said, switching his head toward fat, pig-tailed Mary Andover, whose blue eyes immediately bulged with fear, whose pink face went as pale as Marjorie's.

Cousin! About fifth cousin twice removed, Mattilda thought sourly. She looked with sympathy at Mary, thought about her long, long walk to school, the pleasure she took in books.

But now Sarah had her weapon. Take your cousin and go, she could say.

Fast as the thought came, Sarah's pained look at Mary dismissed it. Never in this world would she put Mary out.

Where *was* their father?

"Oh, yes," Sarah said, "I had forgotten Mary was your cousin."

Like everybody else. Especially Mary.

"Well, then. You've got your reason. So now I must consider what will happen to *me*. Will they put me in jail?"

Perish the thought, Mr. Beard's deprecating hand said. He was fixing to bow again or poke his chin out, when Sarah went on silkily.

"Of course, it will have to be *proved* I'm teaching Lucas and Docia to read. Let's see," she said, turning to the class, "Lucas, Docia, would you care to read to Mr. Beard to show what you know?"

There was no answer. The silence hung heavy, broken suddenly by a snicker from Docia. Mr. Beard's face slowly began to redden.

"Why, then," Sarah went on, "would any of the pupils like to tell Mr. Beard that you have seen me teach Lucas and Docia to read?"

Silence. Again a snicker from Docia. Mattilda fought her own nervous laughter. The red crept across Mr. Beard's face onto his neck. He waited.

"Mary?" he finally grated.

Mary sat wordless, as plump and settled as a parlor cushion.

Mattilda's laughter got away from her and caught up other students, started a soft tittering around the room.

"Mary!"

Mary's face was red now, but she kept her head lowered and said not a word.

Mr. Beard hiked up his pants and left, the laughter building and breaking around him. The yardstick in Sarah's back collapsed. "Whoof," she said, and she sat down.

17

The laughter had barely subsided when Papa came in, followed by Bill.

"Trouble?" he said to Sarah.

"Why, no, sir," Sarah said. "But now that we've got you here at last, why don't you listen to our pupils?"

He sat down, alert as a hawk.

"Lucas, will you read?"

The deep rich voice began to read, and the pupils settled to listen and follow the words in their books.

Oh, Lucas reads beautiful, Mattilda thought. He did indeed.

Five

April 1861

The whole family was at the noon dinner table; the twenty-five-year-old twins Bland Junior and Sarah; twenty-two-year-old twins Joe and Michael; Marjorie, twenty-four, sulky because Albert King had not been around lately; Elizabeth, seventeen; and Bill, only thirteen but cocky as a banty; Mattilda, twelve. Mattilda wished Sarah's husband, Jason Fisher, had come to dinner too. She felt a strange mixture of love and shyness toward her big, gentle brother-in-law.

Mattilda sat next to her father, determined to say something about Kanawha and even something about freeing Docia, if she could get up her nerve.

To her amazement her family started discussing Kanawha before she got her chance. Bland Junior and Joe got into a shouting match.

"It's all everybody at the courthouse can talk about," Bland Junior said. "Half the people talking about staying with the Union and the other half talking about going with Virginia if she goes. Talking about splitting into Virginia and Kanawha. I don't hardly know what to think."

"Shuh," said Joe. "I know what *I'm* going to do, I'm going with Virginia!"

There was a chorus of "Me too" followed by "No, sir, not me" from a few voices.

"How does anybody know what's going to happen?" Marjorie demanded, her eyes snapping, her face red and angry. "How do *we* know what we'll do if the Union decides it's going to come over here and take our property from us? Answer me that, somebody."

Property! thought Mattilda. That meant *Docia*. Can people be property? She looked at Luella, Docia's mother, shovelling a second panful of cornbread onto the serving tray at the sideboard. Her face was strained, withdrawn, closing out the white folks. It was time to speak up.

"I don't believe in slavery no more," Mattilda said, trying hard to control her voice so that it would come out full and commanding like an adult's. Her emotion tricked her and her voice squeaked. She faltered but continued.

"I'm a Republican," she said.

The blast of laughter hit her, as she knew it would, but Luella turned and looked at her, a piercing shaft of a look, alive, aware, warm. It was the first time a black adult had ever done this, and she felt on the verge of a discovery of something so great she couldn't comprehend it yet. Luella's look was so strong that it dimmed the hurtful laughter. Ordinarily Mattilda would have burst into angry tears and left the table, but she stayed, stubborn and hot.

A brief secret smile touched her mother's face. Mama was

19

pleased with her, she believed.

Suddenly she had a defender. Sarah edged her voice softly in. "Jason feels the same way, and so do I," she said. "We have slaves because we inherited a situation, not because it's moral. And *I* think it's immoral."

Bland Junior stared at his twin in cold disbelief. Twenty minutes ago he had been overjoyed that his sister had come for dinner.

"Surely, Sarah, you'd not be so cruel as to turn our servants out to fend for themselves, would you? How they going to take care of themselves?"

"Same way they take care of us," Sarah said coolly. "Bland Junior, do you notice that you never say the word slave, only servant? Have you thought why that is?"

Mattilda snickered to herself. That was a good blow.

"You got no right to talk," cried Bill in anger. "What about Elijah?"

It was true. Elijah, a black male, thirty years old, was Jason's slave, although the reverse appeared to be true. It was the family joke that Jason and Sarah got more advice and direction from Elijah than he from them. Elijah neither looked nor acted like a slave. He had a wide wrinkled smile and mutton chop whiskers, which he constantly preened. You couldn't help laughing back at Elijah. He didn't give a hoot about being a slave, Mattilda felt sure.

"Just what I was fixing to ask next," Bland Junior said in triumph.

Mattilda didn't worry. Sarah was little and quiet, a gray-eyed beauty with long red hair wound in a high bun—her cow-plop, she called it when it wouldn't do; her crowning glory, Jason called it. But she was tough as whit-leather when it came to an argument on right and wrong. Oh, Sarah was dear, her favorite sister, Mattilda decided.

"How the rest of y'all going in case it comes to it?" Bland Junior challenged.

Quickly they chose sides. "I was born a Virginian; I'll die a Virginian," declared Marjorie.

"I'm a citizen of the United States," retorted Joe. "Virginia comes second to that."

"Me too," agreed Michael, his twin.

"No, sir," snapped Bill. "Virginia ain't second to *nowhere*."

Bill was only one year older than Mattilda, but they accepted his decision without laughter, Mattilda noted bitterly. Why? Why was his word better than hers?

The vote went around. They were evenly divided, four to four, and still her parents had not spoken. They became silent, pondered, waited, watched their parents, became aware of Luella's quiet presence, watched her. Nobody voiced the questions hanging heavy in the air. Mattilda believed the answer to the argument had already been settled in her parents' minds. Her little bald-headed father had a mild-as-milk look on his face, hiding his sharp decisive mind and *fooling* you if you didn't know him well. Oh, he'd decided all right. He piled gooseberry preserves lavishly on his buttered cornbread and ate, giving a bland smile to his children. Bland Senior was a fitting name for him.

"Anybody going need any more bread?" Luella asked. "This is the last pan of cornbread, and we going whip up some biscuit dough if you want more."

Michael and Joe, long and stringy, reached at the same time for the platter. There was a soft chorus of refusals.

"No, thank you, Luella," said their mother. "I don't want them to get foundered."

"Dorothy, you have outdone yourself with these preserves," Bland Senior told his wife.

21

She smiled her thanks. "Have some more?" she asked. "No dessert today."

"Can't beat that for dessert," he said. "Now, Luella, I want you to tell the servants I expect all of them to prayers in the morning."

His children alerted to this direction. It would be a speech taking up half the day, Mattilda thought. What was it about? Her father never bothered about who came to Sunday prayers and in fact often found reasons to miss them himself. She noted too that like Bland Junior he never said slave, always servant. Slave said too much. It was too cruel. We keep you here against your will, it said, even if there were a pretence that every slave really preferred to be there, protected and loved by his master.

Mattilda left the table, full of food yet hurting from the unfinished, unsettled argument. Why wouldn't her father say his say?

Six

Sunday breakfast was Mattilda's favorite meal, unvarying, comfortable ritual: crisp side of pork, stewed apples, yeast coffeecake crusty with cinnamon and sugar. Mattilda stood at the sideboard and served herself, fending off Joe's long arms. Her parents, side by side at the head of the long table, waited patiently for the twins to fill up.

Finally, "Set the benches up, boys," Papa directed. The benches, stacked in the long pantry, were brought out and placed two rows deep around the table.

Luella went out. "Prayer meeting," she called, her voice drawn out long and thin, as if she were calling someone from the next county.

Quietly, they came in, old and young, anxious and curious about being summoned to prayers, their eyes snapping a look and then turning down properly. Except for Luella and Lucas and Docia (mavericks, upright and unafraid). Mattilda watched the familiar faces, wished she could tell them that all was well. Docia passed and dropped a slow wink, and just as solemnly Mattilda returned it.

Mama read a psalm, and Mattilda tried to listen. "Thy throne is established of old; thou art from everlasting. The floods have lifted up, O Lord, the floods have lifted up their voice."

They were deep words, important enough to give thought to, but Mattilda could not.

Prayers began, Papa's short and to the point: Let us have what we need and let us deserve it. Same thing he always prayed. Her mother called for blessings on them and protection in this time of uncertainty.

Luella prayed then, a bold sudden appeal. "Lord, please make me free. Amen."

Shock. Mattilda's eyes sought Docia's. Whites and blacks were silent, appalled at her nerve. Papa's face was stern. "Anybody else feel moved to pray?" he asked.

Nobody did. Luella's prayer had said enough. Then, Papa stood up. Here came the speech. "You all know, I reckon, that there's a big trouble getting started. Looks like it might get to be a fight, North against South, maybe even come to splitting the country wide apart, God forbid. If it does, I will abide by what Virginia decides for this reason. First rights are human rights. Then comes the nearby government rights. That's the *state*. Then comes federal government rights. To me it is wrong for the country to take away the rights of the states.''

Mattilda's heart grew cold. She looked at Docia's bright angry eyes.

"On the other hand, there is the question of slavery. Mrs. Repass and I talked it over and over and over. First rights are human rights. We can only conclude it is a bad and evil thing to make a person a slave. So we now set you free." His voice had sunk so low Mattilda doubted her hearing.

"What, Papa?" she said with great excitement. "What?"

"You are all free," her father said in a loud voice. "We have written manumission papers for each and every one of you."

It was the shortest speech Papa had ever made, and the best.

"Glory," said Luella. "Glory to the Lord. Glory."

"Luella, you do pray good," Papa said with a sly smile.

She sure does, thought Mattilda. Next time I want something bad enough, I'm going to ask Luella to pray for it.

The hugs went around, Luella to Mama, Mama to Papa, Papa to Willie. Mattilda went around the table and hugged Docia. She wished her sister Sarah were here to be hugged. And Jason. The room jarred with laughter, expostulations, slapping handshakes. Jubilation.

The mood changed quickly. Some of the blacks began to look fearful, especially Aunt Lu, so fragile and old that no one remembered her age. Her hands shook, and her mouth worked. "What we going do?" she asked Papa. "Where we going?"

"Well," he said, "you can leave if you wish with clothes and with twenty dollars for each adult, ten for each child. Or you can stay and work here as before, and I'll pay you what I can." He held up a cautioning hand. "It won't be much money. We don't have it. Your clothes and food will still be

24

same as ours, and you'll get some money according to what you do. It'll take some thinking and working out to know how much money.''

"What can I do?" asked Aunt Lu. "Ain't no kind of work I can do now." Her face was worried, baffled.

"You'll do whatever you can, Aunt Lu," Mama said gently. "You'll help me, or you'll work in your own daughter's kitchen. Or you'll make us a rug. But mostly you'll rest yourself. Deserve it too."

There was an immediate let-go of tension, except in Lucas. "But if we went away," said Lucas, looking young and intense, "where would we go?" Lucas stood solidly, great arms folded, legs like tree trunks. His black eyes blazed with excitement. It was the first time Mattilda had seen him with an emotion other than anger.

"Oh Lucas, I would truly hate to see you leave," said her father. "Where will I get a blacksmith to equal you?" He studied Lucas, saw the adventure in him, sighed. "It'll be hard. You're going, I see."

Lucas tested his freedom. "Bland Senior, if I stay here, it's still going to be like slavery. You know? I got to be new, think new."

Papa blinked at being first-named so suddenly, accepted it with a shrug, went on with the conversation. Only his regret at the prospect of losing Lucas showed.

"Well, you're going. Seems like you could get a job without much trouble. A good blacksmith can get work anywhere."

"Yes, man, as a slave," Lucas said. "Around here ain't nothing but slave blacksmiths. I got to move away from slaveholders. Just point me in a direction, and I'll go."

Prayer meeting was over, but the family and the freed people lingered, some listening to Lucas and Papa, some getting into their own little talk groups, questioning and resolving, changing minds, the blacks weeping suddenly and then smiling, trying to get the *feel* of freedom.

"I believe I'd start in Princeton," her father was saying. "Not many slaves there. I tell you what, I'm going write you a letter to carry, telling about your good work. How's that?"

Things were different already, Mattilda saw. Lucas was only the first. Who would be next—Luella and Docia? She hoped not. It was *different* to see the whites and blacks talking to each other in curious hesitant voices, searching for a balance with each other, the right words to say. A load had lifted, and yet the light questioning voices seemed to miss the old familiar certainties.

"That'll be good," Lucas said. "I tell you, how about if I stay till I teach somebody? You know, get him started."

"Oh fine." Her father looked relieved. "That would help."

Michael stepped closer. "Let him teach me, Papa." It was a new thought. White people would need to learn. Lucas glanced at Michael's spindly body and narrow shoulders, but he refrained from comment. He used to be skinny himself. Besides he had his own learning to do, and Michael might be *his* teacher.

Papa studied and nodded. "You're right, Mike. All right."

Mattilda saw that her mother's face glowed with satisfaction. She had never had such a feeling of pride in her father and in her mother who had, she knew with certainty, been the starter of the whole thing.

Seven

Michael made a nail. Except for shoeing horses, he couldn't get the hang of smithing. Even so, he had to depend upon Lucas for preparing the shoe which he then pounded into place.

Listening to the incessant hammering, Mattilda thought, There's Lucas now, when the sound came like a clear song from the barn. *Tinkety-tinkety-tinkety . . . TONK tink tink . . . TONK tink tink.* And then she braced herself for Michael's pounding. The rhythm became dull and unbroken . . . *tunk-tunk, tunk-tunk-tunk,* until Mattilda thought she'd go mad with the monotony of it. The only thing that saved her from insanity was the fact that she often collapsed in helpless laughter over the sound.

Lucas shook his head over Michael's determination to make a nail. "Be better if you try something bigger to start with, Michael. Lots of wagon work need doing."

Michael always shook his head and doggedly took up his furious whanging again. At last he had a nail to suit him.

It was a beauty, two inches long, square, tapering almost to a point, a good honest nail. Mattilda asked for it and he proudly gave it to her, as if he were presenting a diamond necklace.

Eight

Lucas felt free to go, could wait no longer. He walked away from the house, looking strange to Docia and Mattilda in his good brown homespun coat and his oiled shoes, like a city man. He turned at the curve of the narrow gravel road and waved jauntily. They waved back, and Luella, always so composed, suddenly groaned.

"Oh, Lucas, baby," she said loudly. Docia cried and Mattilda felt her own eyes misting.

Nine

Lucas showed up at the family house, belly-wounded, vomiting and feverish, coat and shoes gone. His eyes glared red with hatred and pain.

Luella and Docia, anguished, hurried in and Mattilda met them at the kitchen door.

"Take Docia up to your room," directed her mother. "Stay there till we call you."

"Oh no, Mama. Why?" asked Mattilda, seeing Docia's agitation.

"We'll be tending to Lucas. You girls can't be there." She paused and patted Docia's shoulder. "I'm sorry, Docia."

In the darkened hall Docia clutched Mattilda's arm, put a

finger to her lips. With quick agreement they slid down to sit in the shadows and wait, watch, listen. It was the only thing they ever got to do, Mattilda thought, watch and listen, never take part.

"The ruckus done started," Lucas said, groaning as her father and Luella cut his shirt away from the clotted wound. "They wouldn't let me get to Princeton. Tore up my papers and laughed. Stole my clothes." Lucas stopped and heaved, wiped his bloody mouth with a bit of bleached sheet Luella handed him. "I got me one of them though. Go tearing up my free papers! I kicked hell out of . . ." Sick as he was, he paused, looked at Dorothy Repass and his mother. "I kicked him good."

Lucas grimaced, pleasure with pain. "He hollered. Lordy." He rested, eyes closed.

Papa eased the bloody shirt, tight as a second skin, away from the wound.

"There now, son," Mama spoke for Luella who gritted her teeth in silence. Lucas subsided, glared at the light. He talked on.

"Other man shot at me three times, all missed but first shot. I was *gone* from there after the first one."

"Who were they, Lucas?" Papa asked, his voice shaking with fury.

"Don't know. White men. This side of Princeton. Don't know who they for, who they against." He sighed, slept a moment, awoke suddenly.

"They wanted to get ready for the fight. Wanted a nigger to practice on. And there I was, handy."

The patch of shirt was off. The light fell full on Papa's face when he stood up and looked hopelessly at his wife.

"Get somebody to go for George," he told her. She lit a candle and left.

It was hopeless, Mattilda thought, if her father would send

29

for his doctor brother. He had never been able to hide his irritation around his noisy, confident, unfeeling older brother, and only during the direst of emergencies would he give in and send for Uncle George. "Come on," she said to Docia, and together they went into the room to wait with Luella.

Uncle George examined Lucas, put out some pills, snapped his bag shut. "You could have saved me some sleep on this one, Bland," he said coldly. "Give him one of these pills whenever he hurts too bad."

He straightened, took his time looking at each person in the room, finally settled his look on Docia. "Come hold my horse," he ordered. Silently Docia followed him into the dark.

Ten

Lucas took eight days to die. His fitful talking and occasional screams put a dark mood over the farm, used as they were to the happier sounds he produced with his maul and anvil. He was the first person Mattilda knew to die, and she tried to think about his death, but her mind skittered nervously away. She couldn't believe he was dead, kept expecting to see him when she went over to see Docia.

Lucas was laid out in Luella's house and was surrounded by great bunches of early apple blossoms. The Repass men worked with the blacks building a coffin and digging a grave. Mattilda climbed the hill when they were through and looked at the orange dirt pile, soon to be shovelled onto Lucas. She felt a grue, like the touch of a cool ghostly hand, and she ran down the hill, falling and rolling, then running again till she was safely home.

Her sisters worked on the satin lining for the coffin, and the freed women prepared the food for the wake. None of it seemed real to Mattilda, not even Lucas lying stiff and military, chin lifted defiantly. It wasn't really Lucas, she thought.

It was at the barn that Lucas was real, because there, every leaning wagon wheel casting its shadow on the board and batten had Lucas's touch. Every clinking noise brought Lucas's anvil song, cheerful and alive, to her mind. Lucas couldn't be dead.

Eleven

May 1861

It was Saturday and the house was in an uproar over preparations for the spring party, no matter that the War seemed to be full upon them. Nobody *really* believed in the War, except maybe Luella whose grieving face kept reminding everybody of Lucas. Except Docia who sometimes broke into tears unexpectedly. Except Sarah whose serious worried look sent uncontrollable shivers of fright scurrying out from Mattilda's stomach to her very hands and feet. The men in the family seemed excited and ready for adventure or for a party.

Mattilda and Docia gathered flowers to put into every room in the house, handmaidens to Marjorie, who did the arrangements. They covered the work table with great pans and crocks full of glowing irises, love-in-a-mist, dogwood, wild azalea, columbine, lilacs, peonies lavishly red and pink, laurel leaves for greenery. They filled bowls with lily of the valley and purple violets, looking very sweet and innocent, hard to arrange, a challenge to Marjorie.

Mattilda's dress, pink with embroidered rosebuds around the hem, ironed to a fare-thee-well, hung by the window in the kitchen where it would catch the cool drying breeze before Luella sent it upstairs. Luella gave a wink when she caught Mattilda dreaming over the dress. It flared all right, but Mattilda did wish Mama would let her have a bird cage—they separated the girls from the women.

"What you going do with a bird cage on a nothing shape?" Docia demanded.

"That's what I mean," said Mattilda. "I'm going to *get* me some shape."

Docia snickered, poked her meager rear out, leered at it sidelong. "I'm going get mine natural."

Mattilda hated the flowers, hated planting flowers, hated the weeding, watering, hoeing, gathering (under someone else's direction—"Mind you cut the stems long now"—as if she were an idiot). Leave it to her and she would cut a great bunch of blooms, plop them into a gallon crock and put them on the table. Then who didn't like them could look elsewhere.

Marjorie arranged the flowers, tilting her head and frowning, then sent Mattilda or Docia with the finished product to the proper place.

"This goes on the mantel in Mama's room, *this* side toward the door," And so on and on till the whole house was sweet and eye-catching, whereupon Mattilda's hatred for flowers unreasonably switched to love, and when she should have been bathing, she was wandering about the house looking with a feeling of pride and accomplishment at the dozens of bouquets.

32

Twelve

The party differed from all the others she could remember when she was allowed to peek from the inside kitchen or from the balustrade on the second floor. The purpose of a party, she had observed, was to get the men and women together so they could dance, flirt, eat, laugh and joke together. This time though the men cavorted like little boys off on an adventure. Ignored the women. Laughed. Clapped backs. Were *joyful*. Mattilda wondered whether the War made them happy, or whether the flowers could be making them as giddy as they did her. Men were hard to understand. Their swaggering courtesies to the ladies could turn to sudden loud cruelty. She watched the laughing group across the dining room from her. She sat near the hall door where she could give hasty reports to Docia, who helped Luella and the other women to get the buffet ready. So far there had been nothing to report, but soon the dancing would begin and she would be struggling not to laugh at the dancers. Would she be asked to dance? And if she were, how would she respond? Docia had told her to give the man a flirty look and say, "I been wondering when you'd ask." She should have asked her mother or Sarah.

Meanwhile she sat alone, not old enough to bustle around being a hostess like her sisters nor young enough to sit on the stairs. She was at an inconvenient age. The room was all movement. Except for the one group of men who talked seriously now, in low voices. It was the War, she felt sure. The War was going to ruin the party yet.

She tried to sort the group out. The man in the middle, Ray Beard, who lived at the other end of the county, still held a threat for her. No matter how often she saw him, even after Sarah faced him down at the schoolhouse, he was a stranger looking at her with sober eyes and a wide grin, so that the top half of his face was a mismatch to the bottom. "And how's Miss Mattilda?" he would ask as if he were checking with a third person, looking without expression in his wide green eyes beyond and above her.

Mattilda wasn't fooled. Mr. Beard regarded her as a little girl, stupid and silly, not a *person*. He acted the same way to the old ladies, she had noticed, treating them with a kind of remote courtesy, a closed look to hide his supposition that they weren't quite bright. When he finished making his manners, he jutted his chin forward, as if he were using it to thrust something ugly aside. Only with men and with the young women did Mr. Beard come alive and real. It was enough to make you hate him, Mattilda thought, and she determined she would remember to keep on hating him when she was old enough for him to start noticing.

Now Mr. Beard talked with fierce intensity to the group of men who had increased in number till now they took up half the room. Fiddle music, smooth as silk, started up in the other room. This was her first party, and she wanted to dance! This despite the fact that she had told Docia her sure answer to an invitation would be, "Why, no, thank you. My corn aches me."

Her three older brothers were now with the group, and the voices had risen, an ominous undertone in them. She couldn't catch what they were saying, oh a word or two about Governor Wise and the new forts the southern states had claimed, but she didn't see the connection.

She wished she could run tell Mama and Papa, but she

remembered well her lesson about the party. "You do not walk around the room without an escort." She was effectively tied to a chair, and it wasn't sensible.

There were two groups in the room, she now saw, one surrounding Mr. Beard and one formless drifting group of both men and women, moving to each other for support, a quick touch, a smile. A leaderless group.

Sarah and Jason smiled and waved to her from the door and she felt a flood of relief. Her parents needed to leave the front hall where they were greeting the guests and come on in here to get the party started, but maybe Sarah and Jason could get it going.

Sarah was beautiful to look at, Mattilda was pleased to note, and never mind who noticed that she was pregnant. No doubt she would get snippish looks for dancing in her condition. Jason, brown as an oak leaf over his snowy shirt, glanced around the room and in particular at Mr. Beard's audience. He bent low to talk to Sarah, and she nodded, lifted her arms to him, and they galloped around the group in a feisty polka that was bound to draw the party together. Mattilda relaxed at once, thankful that they had decided to start the dancing instead of waiting for her father to do the honors with one of his daughters. To his eternal irritation, Mama refused to dance, except to do an unexpected clog to delight her children in the privacy of the family. But dancing and Methodism clashed, she firmly believed, though she never tried to stop her children.

They romped past Beard's group, and Sarah gave Bland Junior a solid commanding thump on the shoulder. His bewildered, angry face emerged from the group, softened at the sight of his sister. He realized at once that the party was dying, and he became a host. "Excuse me, gentlemen," he said. "Time to dance." There was almost an audible sigh of relief from the women who sat together, trying to look unconcerned.

It didn't work though. Bland Junior swung his girl into the dance, and the nebulous floating group tried to get into it but most of them couldn't do the polka, Mattilda saw. *She* could. Why didn't someone ask her?

The music stopped. "Ask them to play another waltz," a man's voice pleaded, and she heard a waltz begin. Suddenly there was Jason, bowing and smiling at her as if she were real and not the little lump on a chair she was beginning to feel like. Oh, she was afraid. She'd do something terrible and all her practice would be for naught.

"Scary the first time, isn't it?" said Jason, looking into her mind. "I remember how it is."

Mattilda decided she loved Jason and that she would go sadly through life forever without a sweetheart because her only love was married. Away they went, and if she was clumsy till she got into the rhythm, it didn't matter. Jason would understand. Quickly though she was into it, gliding with him, away and back, light and happy as a kitten.

Then her father's voice commanded. "Gentlemen, let's get on with the party," a clear direct challenge to Mr. Beard. Mattilda listened tensely, as Jason's firm hand steered her away.

"Bland Senior, we're trying to plan something, get something settled, and *you* caused part of the problem," Mr. Beard said.

Challenge accepted.

Jason led her back to her seat, thanked her (and the waltz not even over yet), quickly moved to Papa's side. Michael and Joe suddenly withdrew from the group and joined the two Blands.

"Well, sir, whatever I have done to cause it, this is not the place or time to discuss it," her father said calmly.

It was strange. All the ladies were around the walls again, in small groups or alone, and all the men were in the middle of the room in two hostile camps, shouldering each other like boys.

"You freed your niggers, sir. Did you consider how that would affect the rest of us. All our niggers sulking up and all?" Mr. Beard shouted into the silence.

Now Papa was mad. He didn't like hollering. "Oh?" he said. "How did it hurt *you?*" The question was sly. Mr. Beard had nary slave nor servant nor even wife to his name. Rage on his face showed that the insult cut deep.

The War was about to happen and right there in front of her. Next thing, Michael would go loping to the parlor for his beloved sword and would come back hacking away with it. Docia's head poked in. "I'm scared, Docia," Mattilda whispered. "They fixing to have it out right here."

"Who's for the North?" Docia asked fiercely, ready to pitch in.

Mattilda was puzzled, couldn't make it out. All her brothers now supported Virginia, she knew, but Jason leaned North and agreed with those who wanted to secede from the secession. Yet he stood with her family. And the floaters too, now they lined up with her father against Mr. Beard. Yet, she believed her father and Mr. Beard sided together, for the South.

Now Bland Junior got into it. "This is the *War* we're talking about, Papa, more important than a party."

But it's my first party, Mattilda thought in dismay.

Bland Junior cleared his throat. "We're going to the courthouse and enlist with Virginia, Joe, Michael and I, leaving Monday morning."

The words were out, and all had heard. They had known it was coming, but the shock on her mother's face made Mattilda feel sick.

"Me too. I'm going too." A clamor of voices and then a silence as Jason stepped aside, his brown face solemn.

37

"I'm going the other way—to the North. I support Mr. Lincoln."

The silence in the room didn't hide the fury in several men near Beard.

"I'll go with you, Jason," offered a short, gray-haired neighbor, "and Billy here wants to go." Thumb pointed at son. Across the room a mother gasped.

The party had split plumb apart in spite of her father's efforts. Mattilda sadly digested the knowledge that not only was Papa not omniscient, but that the War was reaching out for her family. The party was over, before the supper, before the good country dancing had even started.

Couples got together, made their manners to her parents, curiously mixed with their friends who took the opposing side, not yet able to be enemies.

Sarah hugged Mattilda, and Jason said, "You're a good dancer, Matt." The crowd drifted toward the door, talking brightly to cover up the dreadful change in their lives. Sarah and Mama suddenly clutched each other.

"Oh, Mama. What's *happening* to us?" Sarah cried.

It was like a good-bye forever, and Mattilda commenced weeping like a baby.

Thirteen

The morning was bright and clear except for small drifts of mist over the low places, the sun already inhaling it. Mattilda sat on the edge of the bluff where she could get a clear look at Jason and Elijah on the way to meet the Turners, Westfields,

Bradshaws and Kemp Mullins at the fork of the creek and river, and from there they meant to go to Princeton or further north to find a Federal recruiter. Mulehead, patient as Job, waited, tied to a sapling so tender and small that he could have uprooted it with a slight toss of his head. Her family would have laughed at the way she tied him; they thought Mulehead was a joke among horses. She did not. Only she knew his goodness, his willingness to please, and his sharp ability to predict what she wanted.

Mattilda was full of discord: she was lazy under the force of the sun; she was nervous about being the last to tell Jason good-bye (Was that a wife's prerogative?); she was energetic, ready to holler to Jason, mount Mulehead and break a new path down the bluff. Truth was, she didn't know *how* she felt—woeful one moment at the thought of the stupid War and exhilarated the next second at the adventure she was having.

There. THERE! She saw him. No. There were three—four riders, hurrying around the bluff to the beech forest where in olden times she and Docia had spent many a day making play-dolls out of forked sticks with dresses of pawpaw leaves, and cushion chairs out of green moss. A green dim fairyland. She knew those woods well.

Who were these men? She strained to see them, couldn't recognize them. They rounded the bluff, horses' tails swishing in time, and disappeared into the beech grove.

Now came Jason, tall and straight, and Elijah alongside him, talking and gesticulating. Jason threw his head back suddenly and a tick later she heard his laugh, distant and real. Elijah was telling one of his famous jokes. She grinned and waited until they were directly under the bluff before calling out to them. Oh, Jason's surprise would be delicious.

Her mouth was open to call him when the four riders suddenly dashed from the woods and encircled Jason and Elijah.

What was happening? These must be his friends, anti-secession men, wanting to go to Princeton with him. It was clear as a picture to her, the six horses veering away from each other as if afraid of what was coming.

One man, his jaw jutting as if he were pushing something distasteful, nudged Elijah away from Jason and a rope seemed to leap from his hands and around Elijah, pulling him to the ground. Dragging him!

"No!" she heard Jason shout, pulling his own horse in the path of the other.

She should scream, maybe frighten them when they learned someone was watching. A terrible fear gripped her and she could not utter a sound. Now all four men surrounded Jason and he was down.

The fright in her was like a wild bird beating her to death. Her breath wouldn't come. She *must* scream. Jason's horse pranced out of the group, head arched high, tail tossing, prissy as a show horse in this urgent time. Jason was out of sight, but now she could see Elijah, back on his feet, casting off the rope. The four men bent over Jason, hitting, hitting, fists rising and slashing down.

Elijah suddenly leaped for his horse, was on it and out of their reach, riding desperately around them, trying to break through the deadly circle to Jason. Immediately two of the men mounted and met Elijah, one lifting a long gun, taking a slow deliberate aim at Elijah as if there were all the time in the world. Elijah kicked his horse ahead, crashed into the gunman, knocking the rifle aside.

Mattilda heard the first gunshot and the sound released her from her paralysis. She clambered up on Mulehead, slapped him sharply, felt him jolt in surprise and then *go*. She reined him homeward, praying there would be enough men at home to rescue Jason.

40

As she rode, she whispered, "Help . . . Help." A many a time, she had raced Mulehead across the meadows and he had happily run with never a need for switch or slapping hand, but this rocky steep terrain was slippery and dangerous, and he hesitated. She slapped him without pity, her breath returning to her now in great gasps and the tears standing in her eyes, refusing to fall.

At last she was down by the creek and still she slapped. From far back near the grove came Elijah's horse, looking like a rocking horse, jerking along mechanically.

Oh hurry, Mulehead. Slap. Slap.

She kicked the gate latch open, shouldered Mulehead through, left the gate swinging. Her voice returned and she began screaming, "Papa! Papa! Papa!"

They were there at once: her father, her brothers, her mother, the help, all running toward her.

"They're killing Jason. Hurry. They're killing Jason and Elijah."

It seemed to take hours to get horses and guns and all the time she was frantically describing what she had witnessed and urging them to hurry. "Please. Please. Please." At last they were ready. Mattilda, still on Mulehead, turned toward the lane.

"Stay here, Mattilda," her father called. She halted and waited till the horses swept past, all the men, both white and black, grimly silent, and then she followed.

"Matt," called Mama, "come back!" On she went, only yards behind the men.

They met Elijah, strangely humped on his horse, his right shoulder drooping.

Elijah, always dapper and smiling, now had dirt sticking to his sweat and tears streaming down his cheeks.

"Somebody got a pistol for me?" he called out. "You get

me a gun?'' Mattilda saw that his right arm was hanging almost loose and that blood had ruined his good suit.

"We'll get them, Elijah. Go to my house and let them tend you,'' her father said.

"Come on, Papa,'' Joe called out, bursting ahead of them.

"Mattilda!'' Her father had spotted her. "GO HOME.''

Away they went, Mattilda following.

The beech woods were quiet and serene. There was no sign of the four horsemen nor of Jason, though his horse cropped in a slash of sunlight, his neck delicately curved as if he were looking beautiful on purpose. "Jason!'' the men shouted. "Jason!''

Keeping the scrub thickets between her and her father, Mattilda looked anxiously for Jason. She found him.

Jason seemed to be standing taller than usual, his eyes wide and staring at her, his mouth open and ready to speak, his arm held out with a paper stuck in the sleeve.

"Jason?'' she asked, puzzled, accepting the paper.

Slowly, slowly, feet not touching, Jason swung away from her, staring in another direction, ready now to speak to someone else. TRAITOR, the paper said.

Feet not touching! The scream Mattilda had needed earlier labored to escape. It came in gasps and then a little squeal like a caught rabbit and finally a full-throated scream. Even after Papa's arms held her close and safe, she screamed and screamed.

Fourteen

For all her wishing, Mattilda couldn't remember the man's name. She must hurry, she knew. She was holding up the War because her brothers waited till their own little war here at home was over before they rode away.

"Go to bed now, honey," Papa said. "There's no hurry. *Plenty* of time tomorrow."

She kissed her parents good night, went through the living room, tried to hurry past the dark windows near the stairs. A sharp tremor started up her spine and she couldn't go past the windows. "Please," she said to her parents, "close the blinds." Her fear was unreasoning, gripping. She didn't even know what she was afraid of except that it was some unexplainable horror. Maybe a dead man's face suddenly appearing at the window and looking in at her.

Without a word her mother went to the windows and closed the blinds, wood hitting wood with a good safe snap.

Fifteen

Her father's questioning was gentle but persistent. "What does he *look* like, honey?"

"You know," said Mattilda, "he does like this." She thrust

her chin forward. Her father's eyes were blank.

"He doesn't like me," she said. Still no understanding.

"He ruined the spring party," she tried.

She had hit it. Papa's eyes sharpened with realization.

"Beard," he said softly. "Ray Beard."

He was up and on his way. "That would be Beard and Carter and Tubbs," he told his wife. "Maybe Knight was the fourth man."

"Bland Senior, you let the law handle it now, you hear?" his wife called as he left.

Astonished, he poked his head back around the door. "Of course, I will. You surely don't think *we're* lynchers!"

Sixteen

Mattilda dreamed and slept, unwilling to remember or even to look ahead. More than anything, she wanted to see Sarah, but Sarah would not come home, Mama told her, her dark eyes large and anxious. Sarah was pregnant with her first child. She *must* come home.

It was so unlike Sarah, always loving and forgiving, but Jason's death at the hands of Virginia loyalists was not to be forgiven. Nor were any *other* Virginia loyalists to be forgiven and that included all her family, except Bland Junior who switched sides in outrage after Jason was hanged. He would leave for the North as soon as Jason's murderers were arrested.

The War wasn't what Mattilda had expected. Savage and cruel. Neighbor against neighbor, brother against brother. Not a line of courteous men exchanging gunshots with another line of courteous men, each with his lady's scarf pinned over his breast. Nobody falling. Nobody dying. This terrible War was dark and secret, murdering unarmed freed men. From what seemed like a hundred years ago softly came Lucas's music on his anvil.

These cruel warriors hanged men even before they became soldiers. She shuddered away from the vision of Jason slowly turning his back to her.

No thought would stay fixed for two minutes. Too much had happened to shatter her mind into mirror fragments that reflected bits of things she didn't want to look at.

Who was *right* in this War? What was she to believe?

She wished the War were over and done.

She wished she had called out. Maybe Jason would still be alive.

She wished Sarah would come home.

Seventeen

It had gone long past a decent time, and still they waited for Sarah to notify them of the funeral plans.

Mattilda hadn't the endurance to wait, needed to get it settled in her mind, had to pull herself out of the fear and anguish and begin living again. Needed Sarah.

She went softly through the house, avoiding the steady stream of guests who seemed embarrassed at the unseemliness of a family pulling apart at a time when they should be hugging.

Under the flow of solemn conversations ran an electric excitement for at any time now the news of ratifying the ordinance of secession would come. Mattilda understood well enough what it meant. Virginia would be its own country, separate from the United States, just as Docia had told her.

From her room she heard Grandpa Hume, her mother's father. Oh good. His voice went on and on about Virginia and secession. She heard her father's quick impatient questions, heard the high worried voices of the women. What would it mean? their voices seemed to say, though Mattilda could not understand the words.

She waited for Grandpa Hume to come upstairs, knew he would, for they were close friends.

It wasn't long. A quick knock, a rush to her, arms folding her close so that she smelled his good honey-tobacco-wool smell. She clung to him without words.

Grandpa Hume was taller than Michael or Joe, his white hair to his collar, white beard to his chest, his blue eyes shaded by rumpled white brows. He was the only grandfather who looked the way grandfathers were supposed to look.

"We're going to secede?" she said.

"Yes." He pulled back and gave her a sad look. "Virginia is fixing to split apart; the whole *country* will split."

Like Sarah and her family. Mattilda began shivering. Jason, Sarah, Virginia, the country. She had no steady place to stand. She felt herself give way to the tears and confused words she had held back.

"What can we do, Grandpa Hume? What country will I be in? And where will Sarah be?"

"We don't know yet. This house may be sitting right on the line where the split will be. Or maybe Sarah will be in the North country, and we'll be in the South. Or it could be that this house will be in the North, and *mine* in the South."

As her crying took command, she felt cold and numb except for the hand he held firmly.

46

"It's like the world is coming apart, Grandpa Hume. Tell me how to live," she begged.

"I tell you, honey, this is what life is—a building-up and then a dwindling. Sometimes the dwindling comes fast, like now with Jason's death and Sarah's leaving you. The thing to do is to get a hold on the dwindling and slow it down so you can *bear* it."

She cried on, unable to absorb his words.

"Let's go outside," he said. "We can think better."

Holding hands, they went through the crowds of company, all looking at her. She read their thoughts. "There goes Mattilda, poor little thing. She found Jason. And now Sarah's left her, and she can't get over it. *Poor* little old thing."

For a minute she almost enjoyed the attention till the thought, *Oh, it's true!* struck her and pulled her mouth into ugly crying.

Grandpa Hume walked her to the big poplar tree. "You feel that bark, Mattie," he said. She pressed her hands against it.

"Ain't that a rough real thing?" he said in triumph.

"Yes."

What was he getting at?

"Whenever you feel yourself giving in to the dwindling, you come touch this tree and think to yourself, That's still here. It's *alive*. And *I'll* be alive too."

"What if lightning kills it?"

"Then you grieve a reasonable time. And find another tree. Or a blade of grass."

She touched the tree again. It was true. Its hardness had a kind of magic in it. It opened something in her, let her see out, and she saw that the gray misty day had its own special beauty. She breathed the day in.

She held Grandpa Hume's hand and marvelled at its tough reality. If not a poplar tree, nor a blade of grass, then Grandpa Hume's hand would do.

Eighteen

It was late at night and cool enough for a fire in the living room. Bland Senior, in exhaustion, pulled his boots off and left them by the mantelpiece till he could finish talking.

"I been to the law, such as it is, and I been to Sarah's, and I didn't have any luck either place."

"Judge Stinson told me there wasn't anything could be *done* now. Law has broken down. Everybody going into the army, some to the North, most to the South. Nobody to chase them down except me and our sons, and if we get them, nobody to turn them over to. Judge says wait till the War's over, says it might be six–eight months."

Mama looked gray in the face. "What about Sarah?"

Papa blinked sudden tears away. "She wouldn't see me. Had a couple, man and wife, her neighbors, there on the porch to greet me. They felt bad about it. Said she *couldn't* see us as long as we sided with Jason's murderers." He savagely scrubbed his eyes. "How can Sarah think that?"

"Did you ask about Jason's funeral? Maybe there—"

"They've already had it."

"Had his *funeral* and didn't tell us?" Mama's shock displaced her grief. He nodded, and she was speechless for a while.

"Does she know Bland Junior is going to the Federals?" she asked.

"Yes. He stopped by and she saw him."

"Oh, she saw *him?*"

"Yes. He's on Jason's side."

"Where *are* Ray Beard and Bert Carter and Worth Tubbs? I *agree* with Sarah. It's a disgrace to the state that they've got away."

"Down south some place in the southern army."

"Heroes now," she said. "Kill our daughter's husband and go into the army like heroes."

Bland Senior's hands flashed upward in helpless flight. "They're not representative of the Confederate Army. They're renegades. There's nothing we can do, Dorothy. We have to wait out the War and then get the law on them. Then Sarah will come home."

"The War? Come to your senses, Bland. The War may go on for *years*."

Her father didn't reply, but the uneasy shifting of his glance told Mattilda he was afraid too, and that he didn't have control of the universe as she used to think.

Nineteen

July 1861

Her parents had a loud quarrel, unheard-of and upsetting. Shocking. Her father had his mind made up to go to the War, a very frightening idea to Mattilda. "It's a matter of principle. It would be cowardly not to fight," he kept saying in the tone of sweet reasonableness that always infuriated her mother. It made Mattilda mad too, though she couldn't say why.

"But how can you justify fighting to preserve slavery?" her

mother retorted in a strained voice. "Do you intend to perpetuate slavery in spite of the fact that we have freed ours?"

"No," Papa said, sounding as if he were out of arguments and therefore near to anger. "It's a matter of cowardice. Don't you realize we've got to defend Virginia soil because we, by God, are going to be invaded?"

Now he was shouting.

"We have to preserve our rights and our liberties as free people. My grandpa and *both* your own grandpas fought for this freedom."

"But this fight is about *people* like Luella and Docia, not the freedom of Virginia!" Her mother warmed to the argument.

"It's *not* the question of perpetuating slavery," Papa roared. "There aren't that many slaves around here anyway. You know that, Dorothy. The point's not valid. You're being unfair to bring this in. My *honor* is at stake, and before I see a line of soldiers march down that road from the North, abusing us and our land, I'm going to fight." His voice ended in an outraged squeak.

"Of course, you will if they come here. And I'll be beside you throwing rocks. But not GO to war to some distant strange place." Her mother's voice broke. Thinking about the boys, Mattilda realized. The voices lowered, became silent.

Mattilda unglued her ear from the wall and looked out the side window to the southwest toward the cemetery and the hills beyond covered with wheat and corn and grass all the way to the edge of the timber. So quiet and peaceful and unruffled—it was impossible to believe that a real killing war was going on.

"And what about Bland Junior?" her mother began again. "You going to aim a gun at his head if he comes?"

"Now, Dorothy, you know I'll not do that. Bland Junior

sees it his way, and I see it my way. And your position as my wife should be the same as mine.''

Mattilda grinned at her mother's outraged "Hah!" which smoothed away a little of the fright the quarrel had engendered in her. And she had to clap her hand over her laughter when her mother suddenly won the argument with one sentence, "Bland Senior, you old fool-honey, I can't do without you." Then there were loving murmurs and quiet.

Twenty

"Will we ever hear from Bland Junior?" Mattilda asked. "If he's on *their side,* how will we get a letter?"

"We have to wait till a friendly Union sympathizer can bring a letter," her mother said.

"How can he be friendly *and* a Union sympathizer?" her brother Bill asked in his curious changing voice, whereupon Mattilda in a fury hit him in the stomach with her fist in behalf of Jason and Sarah and Bland Junior and Docia. Maybe even herself—she wasn't sure. Whereupon *he* grabbed her by her one long pigtail, and he swung her face around and started to give her a good smack, and then Papa laid a hand on his arm.

"That's enough, sir."

Mattilda burned silently. Nowadays all of them fell into little quarrels as they never used to do.

Twenty-one

September 1861

Mattilda and Docia rode Mulehead down to the New Creek milldam to get the mail. Surely, *surely* there would be a letter from one of the boys. Or maybe a note from Sarah, saying come get her, she wants to come home.

The War was unreal and remote, and Mattilda only half believed in it. Yet everything in her life had been changed on account of it.

She had not seen Sarah for five months, and she was as haunted by this loss as she was by Jason's death. Maybe Sarah's baby had come by now. Or could Sarah be *dead* and nobody telling her?

Docia was changed, quiet and strange since Lucas's death. She drooped around without energy. Yet Mattilda could talk to Docia as she no longer could to her own family. "Don't upset your mama now," Papa was forever saying. "She's got too many burdens."

This pushed Mattilda out of the house and into Luella's kitchen, where her fears dissipated under the quality of sameness she found there: the same pictures tacked to the logs, the same strong soap smell, the same scrubbed table top, the same friendly faces. It was a place where she found comfort, and Luella always welcomed her.

Today was windless and cold, more like November than September, and the sky looked ready to start something. Mattilda was glad of the warmth of Mulehead on her seat and Docia at her back.

They came to the bee gums, which Lucas and Joe had so carefully sawed out in years past, placed between a clover field and a sourwood grove. Some were rough plank gums, handy to get into at harvest. Collecting the wild gums had been a sport for Joe and Lucas, had become a major crop for the farm, but now the gums were neglected.

"Let's stop a minute," Mattilda said. She and Docia slipped from Mulehead, Docia stepping off on one of the log gums while Mattilda laughed, ready to run if the bees riled. But there was no danger from the logy bees, barely moving in the cold.

"We could take on this job," Mattilda suggested, greatly daring. "I bet there's ten tons of honey in there."

"What you mean, take on this job?" Docia asked with interest.

"Rob the bees. Feed 'em. Ever what you do to bees. We can study about what to do."

"Why we going to do that and get ourselves stung to death?" Docia wasn't argumentative so much as curious.

"Well, we got to work. You know that. And where they going to have us work? In the house. And that's where we get hollered at to do it fast and better and do it RIGHT."

"You know, you got onto something this time, Matt," Docia agreed. "Your daddy ain't got time to bother with the bees. Let's stop and get some honey on the way back. Show what we can do."

"And carry it in what?"

"Pawpaw leaves," Docia improvised. Mattilda nodded, and they rode on.

Mattilda loved to go to the milldam. People congregated there, and the War news came there first, and she might hear rumors of what was happening to Michael, Joe and Bland Junior. Their letters would come there.

There had not been a single letter. Yet everyone going out with a Virginia regiment had taken letters to *them*. Naturally everybody expected it to be a long time before they heard from Bland Junior off somewhere in the Federal army, communications having broken down between North Virginia and South Virginia.

They passed the school, closed and sad despite its sturdy condition, the log-chinking as tight as the day it was built. "Best schoolhouse in fifty miles," her father had bragged, the same as he had when they had added a new outside kitchen to their house after which the old kitchen was known as the inside kitchen: "Best house in fifty miles," and Mattilda supposed he was right. She certainly had seen no finer house except her Great-Uncle Michael's home in Wytheville, with its great columns out front. It made the courthouse look puny. But her parents were contemptuous of the house, built with slave labor. (Luxury at the expense of slaves being considered contemptible, even by those few who owned slaves.)

The schoolhouse looked strange and lonesome at a time when school was supposed to be coming to life; should be children out there scrubbing and sweeping, under the firm direction of Sarah and Marjorie. Children used to ride horseback to this school from miles around. Now that she thought of it, she had lost a happy and important place.

"They deserted the schoolhouse as soon as the War got a good start," she said. "Old people and young women keeping up the farm, and young men keeping up the War. Nobody left to see to the young people."

Docia grunted agreement. "Just when I was starting to read good. I miss it. If anybody had told me last year school was closing, I would have said wonderful, good news, glad to hear it and so on."

Sometimes Dorothy Repass, tense and pressured with the extra burdens that had fallen on her, instructed Mattilda to spend her extra time with her reader, speller and arithmetic book. Occasionally she and Docia had a go at it, but she spent more time pondering the scribblings her older brothers and sisters had left in the books than in the lessons. The value of the books was more in who loved whom and who drew all those little devils with forked tails and did the artist get whacked for it? And who wrote all those careful explaining notes that cleared up puzzling lessons? Sarah, she bet to herself. But she was at a standstill. She had read all the readers through, skipping the questions, and had ignored the arithmetic.

Never mind. School didn't teach you how to tend bees. Or how to catch a pike fish.

The milldam was a good place to fish, so they had brought strings and hooks and a box of worms, and they had permission to fish while they waited for the cornmeal. Fish would be a welcome treat. Once Mattilda had fetched home a wonderful long slim pike fish. "Astonishing," her father had told her. It had made a meal. Another time she had brought a monstrous big catfish, which Luella had baked with dressing, the meat white and delicious. Even Bill had appreciated it.

More often than not, the turtles got the bait and hooks. "Catch them, bring them home. Turtle meat's good," Luella told the two girls. But Mattilda had seen turtles turn up their eyes and look at her as pleading as a puppy, and she always gritted her teeth and tore the hook away unless the turtle had swallowed it and then she cut the string. She let all the turtles go.

Patient Mulehead not only carried the two girls but also pulled the pony cart full of dry shelled corn, ready to grind. No money would change hands since Newt Jackson, the miller, would keep out his portion of cornmeal to sell. They wouldn't have long to wait, just long enough for the excuse to fish. Mattilda loved the water rushing over the dam and the gentle curve of the river above. She remembered warm summer afternoons when she had been swimming there with her brothers and sisters.

Where had that life gone so suddenly? She had not been swimming all summer, and now she had nary a brother at home except Bill.

The mill was on a curve at the lowest part of the road that led northwest over the mountain to Sarah's house, and going there had a little of the old excitement of going to Sarah's. The mill was big, part of it four stories and part two stories high. Old and gray weather-boarded. At the river edge the great wheel caught the swift water and powered the mill, a wonderful thing to watch. And there were *people:* the men on the porch and the women in their wagons.

There was a letter from Michael. The first one! Not like a regular letter but scratched out on brown paper and tied with a string.

Michael's handwriting sent a surge of emotion through her, something that often happened because she had a number of points she could touch upon that would send her into a spin of emotional memories—her loss of Sarah, her loss of her three oldest brothers, her storm of fear when her father saddled up to go vote for secession back in May, along with everybody else in the county except for seven people, and everybody wondered who they were. Couldn't be Jason, who was dead. Couldn't be Bland Junior who was gone to war, or any of the men who had spoken openly for the North because they had gone with Bland Junior. To the south of them, across the mountain at Old Place, everybody was *solidly* in favor of secession. Next month on the fourth Thursday there would be a referendum on splitting the state in two, and the continuous arguments pro and con were splitting Mattilda's head.

She tried to decide whether she dared open Michael's letter, but on the mill porch Newt Jackson distracted her, spitting as passionately as if the spit were worth good money, arguing with assurance, "But we ain't going to split the *state!*" His eyes stood out in amazement.

The new state was to be Kanawha, just as Docia had predicted three long desolate months ago, but Newt Jackson said, "It'll all blow over. You watch, the whole War will blow over when people get to thinking about what they're doing." Silly popeyed fool.

"It won't neither, I tell you," a man said.

Never mind that Michael's letter was addressed to her parents, Mattilda decided. She sat with Docia at the dry edge of the milldam and slipped the string off the letter.

"Dearest Mother and Father and Family," the letter said. That means me so it's all right to read it, Mattilda thought. She trembled, realizing she would soon know about Joe as well as Michael, the two long, tall, skinny soldiers, one blond, one dark-haired, marching together forever in her mind.

"Sunday, September the 8th," Michael said. "I spent the day in reading and writing." (Who cares? thought Mattilda. What's the news? He writes as if he'd already written a hundred times.) "It rained all day. In the early evening Joe Laughlin and others left the company and started to General Wise. It is not yet settled who we are, where we're going to be, and who we belong to. We have not added anyone to the company." (I *hope* not, Mattilda thought, remembering the mob of men and horses ruining the front lawn on the day they assembled and formed the company.) "It's a brave good friendly bunch of men. We have three captains, six lieutenants; we got three sergeants and two corporals, then the humble privates, about 120 in all, or maybe 119, because when they muster us, they call 'Michael, Repass?' in the M's and when they get to the R's, they say 'Repass, Michael?' and I

57

holler '*Ho*' to the first and '*Yay*' to the second.''

Mattilda and Docia laughed.

"So I get counted twice. Now that I've written that, I realize how childish it is, and I won't do it no more."

Mattilda struggled slowly through the letter, occasionally asking Docia's opinion on a scribbled word.

"I still don't know where we're going or what's going to happen, except that we have to keep the Federals from passing freely east to west.

"Tuesday the 10th. We got orders to go to General Floyd. Everybody is a little upset about it because we still admire Governor Wise. Joe has gone to the rangers and I miss him."

Mattilda stopped reading and said in wonderment, "The twins have split up."

"We drilled some and tried to clean up but muddy boots sure won't take blacking.

"Wed. the 11th. We left for General Floyd. Had to leave Jones and Freeman at Lewisburg with the measles, really sick."

"Lewisburg!" Mattilda exclaimed. "That's not far at all."

"We overtook a N.C. regiment and those fellows looked bedraggled, worse than we do. Lot of men sick. We got a message that Jones had died. Of measles.

"Friday the 13th. Matt, does this day scare you?"

Mattilda felt pleased at being singled out by Michael.

"A few men got orders to go back and a few stayed all night with Floyd's 57th Reg. Still no news from home. We don't understand why you haven't written."

"Why *we* haven't written!" exclaimed Mattilda.

"Sat. the 14th. We retreated back last night to top of Big Sewell Mountain. I can hear the big guns and I know the enemy has got to be better fed than we are to have the strength to pull them, or maybe more mules. We had mess with

Grayson Company and got well acquainted with some of the men. Especially Dickey, a very clever fellow. Found men from another New Place company."

Who, Michael? Name them. *Tell* me something.

"I'm sending this to the mill knowing you'll be checking. Jake Barnes is bringing it and is going home sick.

"With love and sincerest regard, your son and brother,

Michael Repass, Private."

But why had he not mentioned fighting? Had he killed any Yankees yet? What was happening? Michael put more questions in her head than answers. There was just no satisfaction to be taken from the War.

Mattilda and Docia got the cornmeal and headed home, knowing a letter from Michael would be more welcome than a whole string of fish, even if it hadn't told a blessed thing except that Joe had gone to the Rangers.

Reluctantly, they rode past the bee gums.

"We coming back tomorrow," Docia said. "We'll bring all the pans we can carry, and we'll take so much honey home their heads will turn."

Twenty-two

Bland Senior studied his war maps, his attention undivided by yesterday's news that Sarah had given birth to a boy. Or by his wife's continuous quiet weeping because she couldn't see her first grandson.

Today his attention was still undivided by Bill's urgency.

Or by Abram's anxious look. Or by Mattilda's wonder at his neglect of the farm.

Bill stormed at him, "Papa, what do you intend us to do? Give us some direction."

Their father's preoccupation was dense as a wall. "All right now," he said. "What is it you want?" You're interrupting my work, his expression said.

Abram, true farmer, only black man left on the farm, burst out, "Man, tell us what you want us to *do!*"

"Do?" said Papa, drawing a careful symbol on the map. "What do you want to do?"

Abram worked hard, had to be everywhere on the farm to lend his strength, could not be unsettled by weather or crop failure. But this unseeing, unhearing Bland Senior baffled him. He turned to Bill, laughing nervously.

Bill took over. "What do you want us to plow? And what animals to slaughter or let live? And what everything else on this damn farm?"

Papa used a ruler, drew a light pencilled line from Lewisburg to Princeton. "No cussing, Bill," he reproached, and added absently, "Oh, I don't know. You and Abram decide it."

Abram performed a great shrug and turned away, but Bill beat his fist down upon the desk.

"You've *surrendered,* Papa!" He stomped out.

Her father's eyes were amazed. "What's the matter with *him?*" he asked Mattilda.

She couldn't answer, but her mind was taken by unease.

Twenty-three

A buggy was drawn up to the door, horse still hitched, and nobody was outside. The house was still. "Mama!" Mattilda called. Heavy footsteps in the second floor hall approached the stairs and started down. What was going on? She moved over to the staircase to look up.

She heard a long moan like an animal cry. What *was* it? She ran to the stairs, heard the moan again, ending in sobs. Mama! Something was wrong with Mama!

A tall bearded man clumped down toward her, frowning in his effort to see her. Grandpa Hume! What in the world? "Wait, honey. Shh! Shhhh!" he said. He was weeping.

"What's happened to Mama?" Mattilda cried to him.

"Your mama's all right, honey. But Bland Junior is dead. Died at Carnifex Ferry with an Ohio Company, shot down by a Confederate soldier." His big hands lifted to hide the tears.

"But your mother is terrified. Thinks Michael's bullet might have done it. God help us all. Poor baby. Poor baby." He cried openly, thinking of his grown-up daughter hurting over her own children. In a moment he straightened himself and held Mattilda again.

"Dorothy can't find Michael's letter that would show it one way or the other." He hesitated. "She dare not ask your daddy."

Mattilda understood. It was an open admission that her father was different, was becoming strange.

Mattilda had not cried when Jason died and she did not cry

now. She trembled and feared that if she left Grandpa Hume's safe arms, she would begin breaking to little bits and would shatter to the floor like a china cup. Upstairs, Mama cried unceasingly and sometimes Papa talked softly. Elizabeth and Marjorie and Bill were undoubtedly crying in their own rooms. And Sarah, Bland Junior's twin, did not even know he was dead, nor had he ever seen her son.

Mattilda felt her mind slipping. She looked across the room at the shelves filled with Bland Junior's collection of little wooden dancers. The dancers' faces suddenly came alive and twisted and distorted, mouths awry with grief. One face solidified into Jason's poor dead face, staring away and away.

Grandpa Hume lifted her face, his blue eyes searching her mind. He led her to the big leather rocker, held her on his lap.

"Mattie, you remember when we talked about dwindling?"

She shivered, nodded.

"Families run the same way," he said. "They got a force that builds and builds and strengthens till it hits a kind of top. And then it starts to dwindle."

Mattilda heard her mind whimpering—Yes, yes, that's our family, dwindling right down to nothing. "Are we all going to die then?" she asked. "Is the War the end of the world?" Tremors shook her whole body.

"No. No," he replied. "It's your *duty* to live."

The old man went on. "The test of the family, the real strength of the family, or the *person* for that matter, is not in the building up but in the falling back."

Mattilda had a terrifying thought. Grandpa Hume was eighty-eight years old. "Are you dwindling, Grandpa?"

He swung her around, looked at her with great astonishment. "Mercy no, Matt. I'm a-building."

Presently Mattilda began to cry against his good Sunday coat, and he held her, giving her a pat now and then. As she cried, she let herself remember Bland Junior and the way he looked the night of the spring party and the way he rode horseback and the way he teased her. The memories called for more tears.

Michael. Pray God he had not killed his brother.

When the grief became almost overwhelming, she found a pure tight untouched spot in the center of her being. She must not allow the horrors get to that.

In the middle of her crying, she caught herself thinking, I don't know how I'll stop the family from falling back. But I'm *quitting* my dwindling. Right now.

Twenty-four

October 1861

Mattilda sat alone on the creek bank. "Mat-TIL-da," she heard Sarah call, a long and lonesome sound from a distance. She turned quickly with a feeling of glad welcome. Sarah was not there. It was something else, the creek water chuckling or the wind brushing a tree branch against the house. Not Sarah.

Twenty-five

April 1862

Joe came a-hollering the way he did when he used to come home from hunting and had got a pair of quail or a turkey, "Hey, hey-hey-hey-HEY EVERYbody. I'm ho-o-o-ome." And it was the same as always: everybody rushed out to see him. Only this time it was a raggedy, bearded soldier, skinny and limber as a cane pole, his behind half out of his pants, his right shoe sole flapping loose with every step. Everybody swarmed around hugging and kissing, and Mama laughed and cried with such noisy enthusiasm that Papa kept saying anxiously, "Hush now. Hush now."

When they finally settled down in the sitting room, Joe told them that Henry Clark had to leave his home as the Yankees took it over. "If you ain't for them, you're against them," Joe said, his eyebrows quirking humorously, "and I reckon they know he's Confederate-minded. So old Henry is out with the Flat Top Copperheads and they're all around the house, but the Feds don't have any idea of it. Haven't the faintest notion they're surrounded."

"Well, where's Mrs. Mize Clark and the children?" his mother demanded.

Joe looked sidelong at her, afraid to tell her. "They're still in the house. Mrs. Clark told Henry to git but she's staying so the Federals don't get the idea the house is theirs."

"Merciful God," Mama said fervently.

"I'm headed for the Clarks now," Joe said. "We're going to get them, all of them. It's going to be a good get-together." His grin was tight and false, and Mattilda didn't believe he was as pleased as he let on. She studied him, trying to see the Joe she knew last year.

"Why don't you write us?" Mattilda asked. "Michael writes us a lot."

"Yes," echoed her mother. "Why don't you write? Michael writes, but then too he hasn't done any fighting yet and I guess he's not as busy."

Papa raised a quick cautioning hand to Joe, but it was too late. Joe's raucous laugh exploded into words, "Michael not fighting? He's fighting all right. His company has done the roughest mountain fighting I know of."

Then Joe caught his father's wince. "Oh. Sorry, Dad. Sorry, Mother. I thought you knew." Mama had turned white, whether from fear for Michael or from rage at being protected from the truth, or whether from the added threat that Michael may have killed Bland Junior, Mattilda couldn't judge. A silence fell over them as they allowed her time to get control. She didn't say a word, but Papa would hear about it later, Mattilda knew.

Why didn't Mama ask Joe about Michael? *He* would know whether Michael had been at Carnifex Ferry. The strained look on her mother's face was answer enough. She was afraid to learn the truth.

"Well, I'll try to be better about writing," Joe finally said. He turned slowly to study his family. "Why, Matt, you're getting to be a beauty." Her embarrassed pleasure was acute.

"You too, Docia."

"Thank you, Joe," Docia said with unstudied elegance. "Who's getting to win the War?"

"Why, we are," he said. "Does that make you mad?"

"Shuh," said Docia tartly, "I don't believe it. Right will win." Everybody laughed, including Joe.

"Honey, run get my guitar," he suddenly begged Mattilda. "I been dying to get my hands on it."

It was no trouble since she kept it in her room and often tried to tease a tune out of it, without much success. Joe picked at it softly while they talked and then went into a song she had not heard before: "I hear the distant thunder hum, Maryland, my Maryland!" She got caught up in the force of the song and when he came to the end each time, she sang "Maryland, my Maryland" with gusto. His strumming sounded like a bass drum, and Mattilda became homesick for a state she had never seen. She began to feel happy the way she used to.

Then Joe picked a quirky little tune, singing the words toward the end, "Who should walk by me, but a young Indian lass." Mattilda loved it, but "Maryland, my Maryland" returned powerfully into her mind the minute Joe stopped singing.

His visit had to be short, and their mother began worrying him about his clothes. "Why don't you take some of your old britches?" she asked. "And a sweater?"

"No, these pants are uniform, even if they're a little thin. I got to get some boots though." And with quick leaps he mounted the stairs, returning in a few minutes wearing some old boots of Michael's.

"Perfect fit," he exulted. "You wait, old Michael will come along wanting these boots before long because he walks while I ride mostly."

"Ride what?" asked his father. "That horse ain't going take you far."

"Ride the railroad train *and* my horse, and he likes to ride the train better than I do. They send us tooting up and down the valley, wherever there's any excitement, just to see we don't miss anything."

Their mother handed him a black sweater. "Take it. You can tie it around your waist to hide your seat as soon as those pants give out." He grinned and accepted the sweater.

For a scared moment Mattilda thought everybody was going to get sad. But then Joe stood briskly and said, "Got to go."

The quick hugs went around again. "Joe, you watch out for Mrs. Clark, hear me?" Mama said. "And you let us hear from you. We worry, you know. Can't help that."

"I will. I'll send word back about the Clarks, first chance." Suddenly Joe looked young and sad. "Tell old Michael hello when you see him. All right? Sometimes I wish I'd never left that company."

And then he was on his thin white horse and pulling her out toward the road. He shifted around on one hip and saluted them and for a while they stayed there watching and listening while the *clop-clop* faded. More slowly, "Maryland, My Maryland" faded from Mattilda's mind.

Finally there was only emptiness and quiet where Joe had been.

Twenty-six

May 1862

Hollering "Hellooooo," from the yard like a mountaineer, Newt Jackson waited for them to come out, refused to step a foot into the house since finery threatened him. "Well, I'm here with the news," he said, bulgy-eyed with importance, "and Joe sent me. He's doing fine himself, but we done took a beating up at Clarks' house." Newt puffed and sucked his teeth, seeing the complete attention he had, enjoying telling it, never mind their anxiety to know fast what was happening.

Um-humm, Mattilda thought. The war wouldn't amount to much, eh?

"What about Mrs. Mize Clark?" Mama asked, unable to endure Newt's slowness.

"I'm getting to that," he said reproachfully. "Well, the Federals was in the house, about seventy-five of them. Imagine that? Sleeping all over the floor in every room, I reckon. And we was all over the woods waiting for them to come out of the house and then we was going to get them."

"We?" Papa said dryly.

"Well, you know, the Rangers and all, two–three companies of our men. At daylight the Federals came out for roll call, lined up in front of the house, scratching theirselves and buttoning up their shirts and yawning and all."

"Get on with it, Newt," Mama burst out. "What about Mrs. Clark?"

"Well, somebody started shooting, before they was all out, too quick, you know, so they all ducked back in the house and commenced a-banging away. Yankees chunked their rifles right through the log-chinks, so they had the best of it because our boys couldn't shoot through those big logs, and Mrs. Clark and her two little ones still there through the whole thing, laying on the floor, I bet, and it going on for *hours*.

"But the Yankees had got the word out somehow, and they stirred up their troops and more Yankee troops started coming in. I tell you, the Federals are on the march. So our boys took leave of the Clarks' place and headed south and tried to stay in Princeton but the Yankees pushed them out and now our men are a-coming. Right this way. Well, not down *this* road, I reckon, but down the turnpike. They're on the march.''

Newt loved the sound of that. "On the march. All of them are on the march.'' He paused to see that he had their attention. "But what's worse, a lot worse, is Princeton, is what they done to Princeton.''

What? What? Mattilda had a sudden terrible vision of all the Princeton people lying dead in the streets. She loved to go to the city of Princeton, was impressed with the great number of houses there, over a hundred she reckoned, although Princeton's dressy people made her feel like a country girl.

"They set Princeton afire and she's a-burning to the ground right now.''

He got the reaction he intended. "No! No!'' cried her mother.

"Well, damn the Federals!'' Papa roared. "Damn such savages!''

Newt Jackson was embarrassed.

"Uh, it was the Confederate troops done it,'' he said. "They got their stores out, what they could, and then burned the houses so the Federals couldn't use them.''

"You see?'' Mama said in a fury to Papa. "That's what war is. No matter that Princeton is mostly loyal to the South. You trying to tell me we ought to be on the side of people who did this?'' Papa was in the way of her urgent need to punish somebody for burning their friends' houses.

She paused, looked sick. "Surely Joe wouldn't take part in such a thing?''

Newt Jackson provided comfort. "No, ma'am. It was the regular company stationed at Princeton, ordered by their colonel.''

"Where are the people who were burned out?'' Mattilda asked.

"On the pike too. Heading for Rocky Ford or Wytheville to relatives or anybody that'll take them in. They're on the way south."

They came stringing down the road; women and children, old men, carrying blankets and food. One man was laden as a mule with cast-iron pans, a flour sifter, tin pans, a colander, tin cups, gourds, all tied to his body, around his neck and waist, draped with string over his arms, clacking and jangling so that they heard him first and thus knew some of the refugees were on New Place Road. All of them wore extra garments, though it was warm, and one young woman had her good hat perched atop her sunbonnet. Some wore Sunday shoes strung around their necks like necklaces. An old woman carried a ham under one arm and a bag of salt under the other. Five candles stood upright in her apron pocket. There were a few carts, hand-pulled, and a couple of wagons pulled by horses.

With the refugees came Confederate soldiers, in no fear or hurry, walking out of step, talking grimly. In moments the front yard was full of people and there was a push to the well at the side. Mama ran out with tin cups. The gourd dipper was not fine enough for Princeton people who had lost their homes nor for the young soldiers either.

"Stop and rest!" she cried. "Come in and sit awhile and tell us about Princeton." The house filled up and it became obvious that they were to have a full house to bed and board that night. Some of them drank and rested in the shade and started on, but others gratefully accepted the Repass hospitality. "Feed my family tonight and in the morning and take this ham in exchange," said the old woman, her pride hurting to ask. Mattilda felt a rush of sympathy. The old woman had swapped places with her and now wore a look of humility, much as she herself used to wear in Princeton.

"Why, no indeed, I'll not take that big ham. You're more than welcome," her mother said quietly. "Come on in."

Mattilda and Docia studied the shock and fury and fatigue on the faces and felt angry too. "Matt," whispered Docia, "say what you will, Federal soldiers would never do that."

"They would too. The War has made everybody crazy."

"Princeton is burned to the ground," a woman said. "Less than a dozen houses left. As we walked out, the Federals walked in." She sighed. "They'll use what's left, I guess."

"They're on their way," another woman said.

"Here? What they want this way? What's down here?" someone asked in puzzlement.

"I'll show you," said Papa, glad of a chance to show off his maps. He led them in and pointed to the Virginia and Tennessee Railroad, where it ran and where it was vulnerable. He pointed to the lead mines at Wytheville and to King's Salt Works.

"Who cares about salt? We have plenty of salt," Mama said in wonder.

"Enough for next winter's meat?" he asked grimly. "Enough for the Confederate army?"

She looked stricken.

Their food stores decreased noticeably during the next few hours, but then their guests all moved on except for Aunt Anna Bailey, old and deaf, who had been burned out of her tiny house where she had lived and cared for herself for almost sixty years. She must find her a new home.

Later they heard there had been a skirmish and General Marshall had drawn his Federals out. And then there was a battle at Lewisburg, and again the Yankees were repulsed.

They began to breathe a bit more easily. But the salt works and the lead mines and the railroad were still there, and in Mattilda's mind there was always a threat of seeing great

71

crowds of people coming down New Place Road again. Next time, she bet, it would be men in blue uniforms, riding four abreast, with bugles blowing and drums beating and flags waving.

Twenty-seven

Mattilda, Docia, Papa, Abram and Grandpa Hume stood in the breezeway by the kitchen and tried to settle a problem.

Mattilda carried the burden of the argument against her father and Docia concentrated upon Abram. It kept things almost equal—white against white and black against black, Mattilda thought, though it wasn't fair in another way. It was hard to fight a man, especially an older man, because he *knew* he was right, and there was never a question or condition in his voice. Thank heaven Grandpa Hume was there as judge.

"Sheepshearing is a hard, high skill job, Matt," her father said kindly. "Harder than beekeeping. Not the sort of thing girls can do."

Girls! Get back into the kitchen, he meant. Sweep the porch. Carry out the mop water. Scrub the pans and skillets. Make up the biscuit dough. And so on. She be damngone if she'd do it.

Mattilda kept her own voice as sweetly reasonable as her father's. "We're just like anybody else. We got to *learn* how to shear a sheep. Then we can do it."

"That's right," Docia told Abram. "Used to be *you* claimed we'd get stung to death if we robbed the bees. But here we stand." Mattilda had a quick memory of Docia that first time. Face so swollen she could barely see.

72

"Lord help," Abram told her. "And you brought a tubful of honey in with a million dead bees floating, and everytime I had honey on biscuit, I had to look and be sure I wouldn't get no bee bones in my teeth."

"That's true," Papa told Mattilda. "Remember all that messy honey?"

"That was our *first* time," Mattilda protested. "How'd *you* do on your first time?"

She was struck by another thought. "Or did you ever learn how to rob bees?"

It was a telling blow, too cruel, she saw, because her father erased all expression from his face to hide the truth, and Grandpa Hume, still apart from the argument, pulled his mouth down to keep from laughing. She bet old Bland Senior never robbed a bee gum in his whole life. Now she tried to remember anytime she had heard him talk about his sheepshearing ability, but she could not.

"The boys are gone except Bill, Papa," she said gently. "Somebody's got to help you all with the farm work, and we're offering."

The nobility of the offer was transparently false, she realized, as everybody knew full well that Docia and Mattilda had turned their minds away from housework.

Abram was still rankled. "What I ought to do is bring a sheep here and let them shear it," he said. "They'd learn soon enough."

"Good thought," Grandpa Hume said, and Abram was away at a run, as anxious as Bland Senior to prove the girls wrong. He brought back a huge sheep, as docile and floppy in his arms as a rag doll.

"It's a way to settle the argument," Grandpa Hume said. "If they can shear this one, let them take up shearing. If they can't, don't let them."

God pity that poor sheep. While Mattilda wrestled to hold him down, Docia whacked at him with the good Sheffield shears, drawing blood and loud cries from the sheep, groans and sweat from themselves. The three men watched silently. When Mattilda was exhausted and matted with sweat, dirt and tears, Docia held the sheep awhile. Who would have guessed a sheep could buck and kick like a contrary mule?

Crying and cutting, holding a leg even after it pitched her, Mattilda worked away, yelling *Ooooh* when she nipped the skin, almost in tune and time with the bleat. She didn't consider giving in. It was a life-death struggle for her own self against her father's notion that she could not shear a sheep.

At last they let the sheep go and picked up the scattered bits of wool. Abram chuckled to himself. "Call that shearing?"

"Yes, I call it shearing," Grandpa Hume said. "What was wrong with it?"

"They didn't get all the wool. They started at the hind end and that's the wrong way."

"How do you know that, Abram?"

"My daddy was the best shearer I ever knew and he showed me how."

"Oh, so you were *taught?*" Grandpa Hume gave Papa some thinking time. "Yet we allowed these two young women to struggle through their first shearing without a single hint about how to do it."

Papa looked away to the mountains. For help, Mattilda imagined. "Abram," he said finally, "let them rest awhile. Then teach them to shear."

Grandpa Hume was a natural teacher, Mattilda thought. He had let Papa learn a good lesson. She remembered watching Grandpa Hume with the boys when they were squaring the logs to build a smokehouse. They hacked away till he said, "Do it the easy way, boys. Don't *slit* it off. Hew against the grain of the wood, and then *lop* it off.''

There must *surely* be an easier way to shear a sheep, and though she wished Grandpa Hume could show her how, Abram would do.

Mattilda's relief at winning was tempered by her father's closed look. The victory had somehow sent him deeper into dwindling. She could not understand why. He would go back to his maps now.

Her mother stuck her head out. "Will it ruin your hands, Mattilda? You're soon coming to courting age, and the sun is already working on your skin."

Mattilda had a qualm about courting. She hastily looked at her hands, as silky as a glove, and triumphantly she held them up, glad to show them because her mother had aroused her worry about whether she'd ever have a sweetheart. Sometimes she looked at herself in the mirror and tried to believe she was pretty, but then in the next minute she would see one of her sisters and would know better. She sighed. If it wasn't her father worrying about her, it was her mother.

Now that there were sheepshearers on the farm again, cloth making could go ahead, and her family would not have to wear the crude sheepskin coats that were becoming so common.

She and Docia lay back on the grass and rested. Why had Papa commenced dwindling again? Mattilda recognized the signs, even if she couldn't understand. She herself had a definite feeling of growth and health.

Twenty-eight

January 1863

"Do you know what freeing the slaves meant to me?" she asked Docia.

"Sure do," Docia answered promptly. "It meant having to empty your own chamber pot."

Half-tickled, half-irritated, Mattilda retorted, "You never had to empty my chamber pot. I did it myself."

"Yes, except when you skipped a day, or when you emptied it into the ferns to keep from walking back to the privy and the ferns died, and so they gave me the job."

"Oh," Mattilda was chagrined. "I'm sorry. I didn't even notice that."

"I forgive you," Docia said magnanimously, having worked her own anger out. "Now what was it about slave freeing?"

Mattilda's embarrassment had chased away her thought. To *think* she had been that spoiled. Slavery was a bad thing.

Twenty-nine

June 1863

Mattilda had been up and down the stairs a dozen times, was puffing from the exertion of it, was angry at Marjorie for not coming downstairs. After all, it was *her* wedding, not Mattilda's, and she should be there to help.

Marjorie bent over her loom, moving with furious energy, producing a blue and white blanket, nothing so special that it couldn't be done later, or even completed by somebody else.

"Why don't you come down and help us with the altar?" Mattilda said. "You going to work on that cover till time for the wedding?"

Marjorie wouldn't answer, kept her head down and worked away. "What did Mama want?" she asked.

"Will plain white sheets be all right to cover the altar?"

"Fine. With flowers around the bottom. And two pillows for kneeling."

"All right." Mattilda started back down, thought better of it, came back to give Marjorie one more try, though Dorothy Repass had said to let her be. "Marjorie, do tell me why you won't come downstairs. You've worked for eight hours on that thing now."

Marjorie gave her a quick shy look. "It settles my agitation."

"Oh."

She went downstairs, pondering that Marjorie, always so

sure and loud, had gone shy and agitated. So Albert King made her nervous. Or getting married did. Whatever it was, Mattilda intended never to get herself into a marriage.

Thirty

July 1863

Ashes to ashes, dust to dust. Over and over the words went through Mattilda's mind. Yet there were no bodies to bury, no ashes, no dust, only the regretful letters saying Michael is dead, Albert King is dead, killed within minutes of each other at the Piney River Crossing in Raleigh County.

Who would swap a Piney River Crossing for Michael? Or *all* of Piney River and the land it touches? Not Mattilda. Not Mama. Mattilda's breast ached with the pain of losing Michael.

Her mother sat holding Papa's hand on her right, Marjorie's on her left. Marjorie's other hand clutched Bill's hand. Mattilda sat on the right end of the hard pew, trying to listen to Brother Sheffey, trying to coax her grief out into the open where it would hurt less. It was a great honor to have Brother Sheffey there, she knew, needed as he was over the whole area, and everybody except herself listened earnestly, raptly, as if the two deaths had given them an excuse for a kind of ecstasy.

No. She would have her own quiet service for Michael. Warm wind made a draft through the open windows, and a June bug lurched through, followed the draft out again.

Michael would never see another June bug, never feel the wind go through the church. She tried to rouse her grief, thinking of this, but she could not even bring Michael's face back. She half heard his laugh, half saw him stoop suddenly, half felt his arms scooping her up, but each impression swooped away, fast and soft as the wind's touch.

The funeral preaching was too distracting and she could not pursue her grief. She must wait till she was alone.

Mattilda watched Marjorie's gloved hand lying quietly in her mother's. Unlike her mother who bent and sobbed aloud, Marjorie seemed composed, more than she did the day before her wedding. Her pregnancy, known only to the family, had given her dignity. Albert King had had just enough military leave to marry her and get her pregnant and then had gone off to get himself killed before she had begun morning sickness. Mattilda had a sudden memory of her embarrassment when Grandpa Hume and Bland Senior fetched Marjorie home from the little house she was fixing up for Albert. Marjorie's white, sick face had moved her to say *something,* but she couldn't think what to say or do. Marjorie had understood. "It's all right, Mattie."

By the end of the funeral service everybody in church was under the power of Brother Sheffey's words, and tears flowed except from Mattilda's and Marjorie's eyes.

But then at the benediction, when it struck Marjorie that there was no funeral wagon to wind around and around the cemetery hill, no bodies to bury, that lost somewhere were two unmarked graves, she cried out, "Is this all? You mean this is ALL?" And she broke into noisy sobs.

Mattilda understood the feeling of unfinished business, the doleful question mark left in the mind.

She slipped away and climbed the long hill to the cemetery. Neglect had beautified it, wild roses and lilacs lying rampant across the graves. She found a spot of red ground free of anthills and sat down to coax her grief out, to relieve the tightness, the hot dryness of her eyes.

Near her, a groundhog burrow went deep into the ground with a pile of discarded pebbles and roots at the entrance. There was a small smooth stone the same red color as all the larger jagged rocks lying about. She picked it up, went into shock as she realized it was a human knee bone just like those on the skeleton she had seen so often in Uncle George's office. After the shock, *fury*. "Hateful groundhog," she said.

Whose bone could it be? It was equidistant from her great-grandparents' graves and several others. She considered keeping it. No, that wouldn't do.

"What do you think of this, Michael?" she asked aloud. She plainly heard him laugh, and she snickered a little too.

Then she knew what to do with the bone. She dropped it back into the hole, bowed her head to unfasten the neck chain holding Michael's nail, dropped it in with the bone, sprinkled a handful of dirt over it. "Ashes to ashes, dust to dust," she said. Suddenly she saw Michael clearly, watched him hammer out the nail, saw his thin determined face.

"I'm sorry you died so young, Michael," she told the image.

At last her grief came full flow and she cried away her pain. Then she packed dirt into the hole, marked the place with a stick and walked down the hill with a feeling of rightness and completion.

If Sarah were here, she could tell her about the bone and hear her laugh the way Michael did.

Thirty-one

Mattilda worked at the loom and Docia at the wheel in the sitting room under the stairwell where Mattilda had insisted the loom be placed, once she and Docia had undertaken the gigantic job of cloth making from sheepshearing to homespun.

The heart of the house was the stairwell. From here Mattilda could glance into her father's office and see him peering through his magnifying glass at his war maps. His bald head gleamed under the light from his coal oil lamp, and his steel spectacles hid his eyes. No question about it, the War had started Papa to dwindling. But it was worse since Michael's death and since his slowly dawning realization that Virginia was losing the war.

Here Mattilda had the stairwell to holler up if she wanted to and the sitting room to enjoy because here was the evening activity, the apple eating and corn popping and walnut hulling, along with the talk. She could see through the double doors into the parlor on those occasions when Elizabeth had a caller, usually a young Confederate mountain fighter at home for a day or two. Elizabeth had become the most beautiful girl in the family, tall and slim, her blonde-red hair pulled smartly back, her eyes as blue as Grandpa Hume's. Sometimes the parlor was filled with visitors who came to exchange sympathy and talk about the War Dead.

On the loom Mattilda used a natural white and a pokeberry red warp with a natural black woof, picturing a beautiful dark suit for her father who had not had one since the War began,

81

although his good smooth suit hung on him like limp ruffles. So bone thin, she thought. He had not had a really happy day since that joyful one of slave freeing, she believed.

She began brooding about changes the War had brought. The house *seemed* the same, but close examination showed that furniture and brass needed polishing; the grass was so tall around the house it would take two days with a scythe to clear it; fields that should be yielding corn were overgrown with brush, and the cattle had become rangy and half-wild. The people were quiet and subdued, sometimes angry without warning.

A lack of care was evident over the whole farm, partly because of a lack of labor and partly because of the despondency of her parents. Mattilda was slowly coming to an understanding of Grandpa Hume's word dwindling. Her papa was dwindling. Despite his hard work and best intentions to keep the farm in good order, his whole aim now was in recording the war maneuvers of the regiments of his sons and his son-in-law.

On the north wall where he could see it from his desk, Papa had a great map of Virginia labeled MICHAEL'S MAP, and at night he studied this map and considered where Michael had been. And why Michael would have lived, if the War had been conducted differently. Mattilda half wondered whether her father thought Michael was alive, whether he found too unbearable the thought that his twin sons had been split by death.

Right now, he followed Joe's progress and talked aloud about it. "Here goes the river and at this bend there must be a bluff. The country is rough here for a thousand men to get through." And so on. And sometimes he argued aloud. "Those damn fools, they can't win there. They shouldn't try that." And a few minutes later, he said, "See? See? I told you it would go wrong."

82

At these times when her father studied the maps, he seemed older than Grandpa Hume, less aware of the realities facing them on the farm. Grandpa Hume stayed at New Place now, using the room next to Sarah's empty room, and he had taken charge of the farm, although no one ever admitted this aloud.

Mattilda worked swiftly with the loom, deeply pleasured by the material she created, though she would never equal Marjorie in skill.

Out of the corner of her eye she saw her father go to Michael's map. He leaned back to study it through his glasses; than he returned to Joe's map. "I see what they're trying to do here," he said to himself. "This must be the road alongside the creek. The line of defense has to go here." And he stopped to draw lines symbolizing breastworks. Thus he spent evening after evening, mostly ignoring Bland Junior's map which was very small and marked with uncertain dotted lines, not that he thought of Bland Junior as an enemy but not much news came from the Yankee side.

She thought about Michael's map, the most complicated of all, because he had written home more than the others. She stretched to relax from the weaving, hated to stop for even a minute, but knew she would soon start to make mistakes. It had become an obsession with her, watching the woolen goods come into being before her eyes, and her satisfaction was deep. Papa looked small and old, bending close to his work, hampered by the poor light. Mattilda studied his face a moment, decided to join him for a while. Docia worked away at the spinning wheel, deep into her own thoughts and free enough with Mattilda that they didn't need to chatter to each other.

Mattilda draped her arm around her father's shoulder, and he pulled her close. "Look at this, honey," he said, pointing

83

to Joe's map. "Joe and Michael were only miles apart when Michael died. It's a wonder he didn't hear about it."

Mattilda leaned forward in great excitement. "What do you mean, Papa? Are you sure?"

"Certainly. Got the letters to prove it."

She looked up at Michael's map which was marked in confusing detail in pencil and blue ink. There was a star at Lewisburg which Michael had mentioned in the first letter they got from him, the beginning of the journey. She remembered the day the letter had come and the elation she had felt when she knew it was from Michael. Lewisburg to Meadow Bluff to the top of Big Sewell.

Papa had drawn a ring surrounded by a circle of sticks like a child's picture of the sun, and that represented Big Sewell Mountain. Retreat to Meadow Bluff. Arrows to indicate the RETREAT printed alongside.

"Missed the whole Carnifex Ferry action!" her father said in wonderment and near vexation.

"Thank God. Thank God," Mattilda cried out. She wished Bland Junior could have missed it too. He would be alive today and maybe he could persuade Sarah to come home.

Unheeding, her father worked on. Mattilda watched.

Here, Michael had written, his company had taken a vote on September 18, 1861, on whether to go with General Wise or whether to go with Floyd, and all but 14 had voted for Wise, and they had started out, but then on September 22nd, Michael had said in great excitement, General Lee had ridden through the camp. Bland Senior had drawn a little box,

$$\boxed{\text{General Lee, 9-22-61}}$$

General Lee settled it that General Floyd was still the man in charge. Michael's company had camped on the north of the hill. *North of the hill—where?* Papa had written in tiny letters.

September 28th, on Saturday, Michael received his first letter from home and Papa had duly noted it down. It was astonishing because they had written many letters.

Rows of tiny rectangles represented breastworks near the mountain top which the "Yankeys" held, and she thought of Michael's labors there, helping to build them. Off to one side, Papa had drawn

Col. Starke 11-15

on the day the colonel had taken over Michael's company. From there began the march to Greenbriar Bridge to Salem or Bon Sacks Depot to Big Tunnel, Michael had written. She tried to picture the tunnel. To Sweetsprings to Potses Creek in Aligainey County. They had laughed at Michael's spelling and had felt closer to him, and Bland Senior had crossed out Alleghany and respelled it according to Michael. To Newcastle. To Catawbie just north of Salem.

At the bottom of the map Papa had neatly asked, *What happened in Salem, Dec. 1861?* and then the response *Dec. 1861—Ordered to S. Carolina.* There went the dotted line to South Carolina where it turned and headed back to Virginia and to

General Field's Brigade.

Williamsburg, May '62. Michael told them he had spent two hours on the grounds of the Eastern Lunatic Asylum by William and Mary College near Fort Magruder. Michael had made jokes about it. It was a good place for his company. The War had brought them to it.

Off to the right were the ominous words *Late '62—Captain Dorman's Company captured at Roanoke Island.* Michael had

told them of prayer meetings he attended with Captain Dorman's company. Men in the two companies had shared food
and had grown close.

May 30, '62—electric storm was printed near Richmond. It
was a terrible storm, Michael had written, flooding the camp
and leaving the clay so soggy it sucked the boots off their
feet.

Then Michael's company returned to western Virginia and
the map around Princeton was filled with a confusion of marks
where Papa had tried to second-guess the generals.

Mattilda thought of Michael's nail buried in red dirt. The
time he made the nail had been a different time, and she had
been a different person. She patted her father's shoulder, feeling that she was older than he was, almost as if she were his
mother. She returned to her work.

Grandpa Hume and Bill came in with a bowl of summer
apples, which meant they would quit work and eat and that her
mother would come in complaining that everybody was up too
late.

Sure enough, there she came. "Bland Senior," she called,
"that's enough time on those maps. You going to win the War
studying on those maps?"

As she talked, Papa and Bill, who were *close* these days,
huddled together. They belonged to the county's newest company, made up of boys under seventeen and of older men. Just
how old, Papa would never say. They loved the drilling,
walked in step together.

"Soon they'll be calling us," her father said loudly. "And
it'll be a desperate measure," he warned his wife, "a last-
ditch try." Mama did not reply, but the desolation in her eyes
was something Mattilda could hardly bear. It was foolish to
worry though. They would never take those boys and old men,
never in this world.

86

Docia went home and Mattilda went to bed, hurrying into her room because she didn't like to look down the hall toward Bland Junior's room. At night it was scary, but she often went into Sarah's room for comfort, just sat there and remembered Sarah till tears eased her. Three years since she'd seen Sarah.

Downstairs she was never afraid, but upstairs she thought of death and dying.

"Good night, honeybunch," Grandpa Hume said at her door.

"Grandpa, is dwindling the same as dying?" It had bothered her for a long time.

"Oh, no," he said without surprise that she would be thinking of this after so long a time. "Dwindling is not dying. It's more of a shrinking of the spirit and a giving up."

Mattilda was greatly relieved. She was not dwindling. She kissed his cheek and gave him a strong good-night hug.

But afterwards when she was in bed, she thought of the change in her parents and the way they seemed to be shrinking out of existence.

Thirty-two

A letter from Michael's colonel sparked Bland Senior into action as nothing else could. The colonel offered his continued sorrow and condolences, saying that Michael was missed by the men, that he had been a mainstay in courage and cheerfulness. Papa sped through the letter, stopping to nod and agree and read sections aloud, saying, "See? That's the way Michael was to them, just like he was to us. A *good* boy." Papa was proud and solemn, thinking about the colonel who saw Michael truly.

And after he got through with the sympathy part, the colonel got down to business, and here too he had Papa's complete attention and agreement. The men of the company, to put it in straight and simple terms, the colonel said, were starving. It was a slow thing, but even if the enemy didn't kill them, starvation would, unless the good people loyal to Virginia gave more food. True enough, he went on, New Place Farm had already given and sold the Confederates more than its share, had been first to send bedcovers (*I* made one of them, Mattilda thought), had helped in a hundred ways to support the cause of freedom of the states. He would not be so bold as to suggest *what* they give, but the need was urgent and would become crucial by fall.

It wouldn't amount to anything, Mattilda thought sadly. Grandpa Hume wasn't here to stir them up. He had left the day before to visit Sarah and to plead with her to come home.

But by the time he finished the letter, her father was on fire for activity, ready to produce the needed food in minutes, not taking into account his long months of neglect. He called together all the adults on the farm, delighting Mattilda with the sudden knowledge that *she* was grown-up in her father's eyes, and they met at the front steps and sat like an obedient congregation and listened to him talk about what they must do. First they went over the food stores, and he winced when he realized how far behind they had fallen.

There was nothing to give.

Next, he got a report from Abram on the crops, on what

might be expected. This was a little better, though great fields were growing up in blackberry vines and goldenrod. "We got wheat ready to cut," Abram said.

"More than we can use?" Papa asked, his head swinging alertly.

"That's not for me to say," Abram said. "You the one always says how much of it we can let go for swapping and feed. But if we squeeze ourselves, ought to be enough for one extra wagonload, if you don't swap it off for something."

"One wagonload it is," said Papa briskly, ignoring all of Abram's hemming and hawing, and taking his final suggestion as the truth. "How about field corn?"

Abram shook his head. "We didn't plant much, like I told you then, and you too busy with your maps to bother. We going to have plenty for us people here, but not for them people there."

"How about sweet corn seed?" Papa asked Luella.

"Enough to plant this farm and two more," Luella said.

"All right. We're going to plant corn in every empty field starting now."

"Plant corn? Now? This late?" Abram said in shock. "Who going to do all that work this late in the year?"

"I am," said Papa. "You are. Mattilda. Aunt Lu. Bill. Elizabeth. Clytie. Docia." He stabbed his forefinger at each one as he named them.

"Me?" quavered Aunt Lu. "Oh Lordie. What can *I* do?"

Papa was his old self, quick and ready. "You'll take charge of Clytie's children and shell the corn and sort out the bad seeds and send the rest to us by the children. Abram and Bill, you'll plow. I want you to start over by the hedge row and plow as far northwest as you can go and turn around and come back, leaving a path big enough to plow later on. Don't try to plow the whole field, just a furrow for planting. When one of you is plowing, the other one will be chopping the big clods right behind him."

"Quicker to harrow," Bill interrupted.

His father paused, looked at Bill. "How many oxen we got, Bill?"

"Why . . . none." Bill looked flustered, unaccustomed to seeing old Bland Senior back. Mattilda was electrified at the change, felt good about her father for the first time in months.

"How many mules?"

"One."

"Right. Now our one mule is going to pull the plow over this whole damn valley. When will we have time to harrow?" He waited, watched the comprehension dawn in Bill's eyes of the enormity of his plan.

"Now we'll leave Dorothy and Luella to take care of the house and kitchen, maybe even the garden and milking if we can't spare them the time."

Mama stood up, brisk as Papa. "All right, lover," she said. She came down the steps and kissed him on the cheek and went with Luella into the house.

Mattilda silently thanked her father for letting her stay with the planting. It would be the first time she had ever done regular farm work, aside from her sheeptending, and she was eager to get at it. Not even Docia showed any objection to working for the Confederate Army, she noted, because she would be working for Michael's friends. But Docia's face was closed and remote. No telling what she was thinking.

Elizabeth, Docia and Mattilda would rake, drop the corn, dip the water. Papa would see that a little wagon carrying water jugs and a dipper gourd were there and ready at all times, for watering the planted seeds. "We *have* to water it," he said. "Can't wait for a rain."

In minutes after Bland Senior's final instructions, they were hard at it, carrying tools out to the field, chopping at ironweed, nobody playing, not even Clytie's two little black children who earnestly sorted the seed under Aunt Lu's urging and then carried good seed out to Elizabeth.

A straight line of red-brown earth climbed the hills to the end of the cleared part of the farm, circled back, leaving an aisle of weeds. Back and forth, back and forth, all day. The little group of new farmers followed. Behind them came the spraddle-legged birds, striking at grubs.

By noon, Mattilda ached from pulling the heavy rake over the rough ground, her shoulder muscles going into little spasms of pain. Elizabeth who had never done *any* outside work toiled with placid face and without complaint, so Mattilda worked on, too proud to ask for a change of job or a rest. She was thankful to hear the dinner bell, immediately stuck up an ironweed to show where the last seed had been planted, started home with the others.

For the first time they all ate together at the big kitchen table, for there had been no time for Luella or Clytie to cook separately for the blacks. Docia looked acutely uncomfortable at being served by Dorothy Repass but shrugged and smiled when Dorothy Repass said, "Oh, Docia, it's not up to Luella's standards. Is that it?" She shook Docia's shoulder gently. So they ate together with pleasure in each other's company and Mattilda took note of it because it was a big thing for her to get to eat with Docia. They winked at each other across the table, and both ate with the same industry that Joe and Michael used to, as if they would never get full. Nobody talked except Papa who talked on and on with great excitement about the yield they would have.

"If it come up at all," Abram murmured.

Papa decreed half an hour of rest, and Mattilda went sound asleep on the porch swing and had to be shaken awake.

It started again, the hard raking, bending, planting, dipping water, straightening with a groan. On and on till dark. Clytie's children and Aunt Lu had the seed all ready in a little while and were excused from further labor, but all the rest kept at it till the bell rang again. They hadn't even gone home to the privy which was not as near as the woods.

Mattilda was thankful that it was downhill to the house, else she would never have made it to the supper table. She barely washed her hands, went to the table with face streaked with dirty sweat. She felt sick at her stomach, felt she couldn't eat but ate with a coming appetite, no longer able to make jokes with Docia who leaned her chin hard on her hands, propped up in half-sleep. They ate, took their dishes to the wash table, thanked Mama and Luella for their meal, said good night and went to bed, even before the cardinals had settled. Mattilda lay awake for a minute, thinking her aches and blisters would keep her awake, then slept. Before dawn, Elizabeth touched her sore shoulder gently, but enough to have her come tearing out of bed, ready to breakfast and go at the fields again.

She began to see her father as a tyrant, but in a day or so, she looked with pride on the fields with the dark furrows. In a week they came to call these days of labor "the time we planted corn," as if it were the only time they ever would, not yet realizing that it was the final change in their way of life. The women in her family now hoed corn.

Thirty-three

August 1863

All the rest of the summer they nursed the corn, walking the rows with hoes and buckets of water in the dry spells. Nobody needed to be told what to do in the morning any more, and going to the fields became routine, except that Mattilda and Docia continued to tend their bee gums and sheep, and Abram and Bill took over the milking again. It was touch and go whether the corn would ripen before frost, though nobody doubted her father's exuberant predictions except Abram who was conservative in his judgments on crop success.

"We don't get frost till the twentieth of October," Papa argued. "As a rule."

"Whew," said Abram. "That's cutting it close."

At last Grandpa Hume wheeled his buggy smartly to the family porch. Mattilda saw him first from the well where she was at the unending job of pumping water to supply the farm. Sorry for herself, she pumped away, waiting till later to talk to her grandfather. In the old days it had been a simple thing to fill up every water vessel plus the tank on the platform against the oak tree, by hitching a horse to a pole pump and letting him walk round and round. Now, however, Mulehead was the family horse, all others having been commandeered by the Princeton troops who needed their strength. So only Grandpa Hume's horse Gray was left for pulling his buggy, the mule for farm work and Mulehead for everything else. And every*body* else. Mattilda accepted this now, with only an occasional display of bitterness at the way the family had forgotten the teasing they used to hand her and Mulehead. Sometimes, when she longed for the old days, Mattilda went to the barnyard, saddled Mulehead and rode him down the road at full gallop, saying silently to her family, "This is *my* horse and I am still the little girl in this family and everything is the same as it always was." All this at the busiest times and at times when Mulehead was needed. But her family watched without comment. Even Bill, who had become manly, was tolerant.

Mattilda pulled the water wagon to the porch, went looking for Grandpa Hume, saw him at the edge of the long, long cornfield with Papa, both of them pulling the stalks over and examining the tops then talking, Papa gesticulating, proud of the work his crew had achieved, and Grandpa Hume shaking his head in admiration.

At last Mattilda ran to Grandpa Hume, enjoying the slapping of her long skirts against her legs. She and Grandpa Hume hugged and rocked, hugged and rocked, his solid old hand beating her back joyfully.

But then. "No, Sarah won't come," he said, his clear eyes watching her in case her grief was too much to bear. He led her away from the house, waved Papa aside.

"There's no way to describe her hurt," he said. "She's hurt and angry that Jason's murderers were never punished. Even more hurt that her own family could take the Confederate side after what they did."

Mattilda's voice was tremulous. "Will she come back some day? When the War is over?"

He considered, shook his head, "I don't know, Mattie. I doubt it. Truly it looks hopeless to me."

He gave her time to absorb this bitterness, went on, "I have

94

a message for you from Sarah. Nobody else in the family is to know. And you're not to tell Docia."

"What? What?" Mattilda asked in great excitement for it was the first time she had heard a word from Sarah.

"She loves you and misses you. And more too," he said hastily, seeing the tears well up suddenly and zigzag down Mattilda's face. "More too. Her boy looks like Jason. She's working with the railroad. Now, Matt, I told her she should think twice about having me tell you this," Grandpa said, cutting his eye toward her in worry. "You *dare not* tell a soul about it."

"Well, what about it?" Mattilda said. "What's so secret about that? Mama wouldn't mind if she worked. How else she going to live?"

She couldn't understand Grandpa Hume's agitation. She was struck by another thought.

"Railroad don't *go* by Sarah's," she said in triumph. "You're teasing me. And *women* don't work for the railroad." She grinned up at him. "It's a joke, isn't it?"

Mattilda worked to keep her grin from breaking because if it were a joke, it was a poor one. It might mean that Sarah had not even sent the message that she loved and missed her.

The old man looked down at her with love. "No, baby, it's not a joke. She really is trusting you with something very serious. She said she remembers how you felt before, and she wants *you* to know but nobody else. The railroad is an escape line for slaves to go to the North and live free. It's not a real railroad."

Mattilda couldn't speak, she was so moved by this new thing about Sarah. She cleared her throat several times.

"How does she do it?"

"She works it through her house. Slaves and freed men alike trust Sarah, and she gets messages to them about when to come, and they send word to other slaves in the South. Get some from plumb down in Mississippi! Then Sarah and her friends hide them there, let them rest, give them food and clothes and head them on north again."

Mattilda's heart was full. Oh, she was proud of Sarah. That was Sarah all right. She remembered Sarah's white and defeated face after Jason was killed, was thankful that she had now returned to herself. She decided that she was a Federal too, as she had been at the first of the War.

"You'll not tell?" Grandpa Hume was still worried.

"Grandpa Hume," Mattilda said fervently, "nobody on God's earth could get that out of me."

The anxious lines on his forehead eased and the sharp look softened. He pulled Mattilda close to him and they started to the house. "That's what she told me," he said gently.

The new thought carried her into the next day when she needed strength, and the assurance that the same old Sarah was still alive in this world supported her.

Thirty-four

October 1863

Everything was fixing to happen at once. The corn was being picked and put into wagons, ready for the colonel's men to come get it. And while they were still hot and sweaty from picking and loading the corn, Bill and Papa would drill with the Home Guard, old men and boys ready to defend Virginia.

And right now while the corn picking was going on, Papa and Mama were having the argument of their lives. The words flew fast and angry across the yard and up to the cornfield, and Mattilda, along with everybody else, listened and waited to see who would win.

"What's the rule?" her mother kept interrupting Papa's steady roar. "Just tell me that one thing. What's the rule on age?"

And Papa thundered on and on about Virginia, about losing Virginia, about fighting against uneven odds, about letting his sons do his fighting for him, about hiding behind his age and so on and so on.

Till finally—

"Bland Senior, you don't tell me the rule about age, then I'll have to ask the colonel's man—lieutenant or whatever he is—just what the age limit is supposed to be, never mind who's listening."

The silence told the listeners at the edge of the cornfield that Mama had won another battle. Having his wife charge him with lying about his age right in front of the residents on the farm and, worse yet, in front of the troops who would soon be there for the corn—that was too much for Papa. Much too much.

Not that he actually *lied* about his age, Mattilda thought. Everybody knew that he was sixty-three. More that he just kept the number fifty out of his conversation, and the men in his company had too much respect to question him. Besides, he kept up with the drilling as well as his own son.

The question was barely settled when they heard distant wheels rolling and the clopping of many horses' hooves hitting the gravel road, and all the corn pickers worked in a frenzy, Mattilda pausing only to look at her blistered and bleeding hands, wondering why on earth she was working for Sarah's

97

enemies and getting an immediate answer from her contrary brain—because they're Michael's friends. It was enough to split you apart.

The soldiers were not yet in sight when they heard Dorothy Repass screaming, "Federals! Federals! Everybody to the house. Run!"

And in the stunned moments before understanding came, sixty or seventy blue-uniformed men, grim as death, their beards hazy with road dust, swept into the yard and around the house, leaving everybody on the farm unarmed in the cornfield, except Mattilda's parents and Aunt Lu and the two little ones.

Every soldier carried a gun, slanting forward and up toward the mountains. They were ready, would *use* the guns, Mattilda realized. She hoped nobody would start anything.

"Fill this wagon next," a squatty sergeant ordered them abruptly, high and safe on his horse. In stunned obedience they turned back to their work, Mattilda in growing terror that Papa would come out with his gun.

And there he came, Mama with him, walking hand in hand like lovers, their eyes black with passion. Thank God, he hadn't brought a gun.

"Sir, are you confiscating this corn?" her father asked the sergeant.

"Yes, sir," replied the sergeant, hoisting his weight to face her father, his horse moving a few restless steps under him. "Your country needs this corn for loyal soldiers, and I know you'll not begrudge it."

Papa was little, but he was steady. "Sir, this corn was raised by Confederates for Confederates, and you are *stealing* it." He paused. "Unless you plan to pay for it." It was a last hope. Maybe they could contribute money to Michael's company.

The sergeant laughed. "Why, sir, we sure *do* plan to pay for it."

Arm out full length, he beckoned with a finger to another soldier. "Give him a note saying the United States owes him for these wagons of corn to be paid in Confederate money upon conclusion of the war."

Papa could do nothing more. Both he and Mama were sick and pale. The way I feel, Mattilda thought, like I'm going to vomit. Still and all, there's no fight.

The private busily wrote the note, grinned at Papa as he handed it over, laughed aloud as Papa read it, crumpled it, threw it down. He turned his back on the sergeant, took his wife's hand again and went to the cornfield. He shook his head at Bill whose fury was taking control. "Everybody go easy," he said. "Nothing we can do now. *Go easy.*"

Mattilda suddenly knew what he meant. Go easy. Don't pick too fast. Princeton soldiers would be here presently.

Orders started snapping. "Get the cows, pigs, chickens, everything. Get it *all*. Get the food from the house. Johnson and Springer, check the house for valuables. Watch for cubbyholes now."

It was unbelievable, and Mattilda *didn't* believe it. They surely would not leave them without food! How do you fight *that?* she wondered.

She began skipping every other cornstalk. She would pick them later for their own use. She dropped an ear of corn, picked it up and tossed it over to Docia in the next row to get her attention. Immediately the two stepped in the same aisle, backs to each other, continued to pick busily.

"Skip a few, Docia."

Docia grunted understanding. Mattilda took a quick glance around. Nobody near. She turned a full stern look on Docia.

"See, Docia? Try to tell *me* Yankees wouldn't treat you

bad. Remember you said that? Yankees are as crazy as Confederates.''

Docia's grin was broken as if her mouth were uncertain whether to express rage or laughter.

"Hurry!" the sergeant called. "Not much time!"

Suddenly a deep voice said in Mattilda's ear, "Pick *all* of it, girl.''

It took minutes to cool her tremors down. She picked deliberately, no longer skipping.

A cow bawled. Mattilda saw with horror that the soldiers were slaughtering the milk cows and heaving their carcasses upon the wagons. Then the pigs started squealing.

Soldiers ran from the house carrying blankets, hunting guns, clothes, food, all in a mess, so that her family would *never* get them straight again, Mattilda thought in confusion. The food went into the wagons, the clothes on the ground. From the breezeway came other men carrying hams.

Black smoke suddenly puffed out of the family porch door, out of the windows, and nearby her family went completely silent, feeling at last what the Princetonians had felt. Mattilda smelled coal oil. Her father started on a run to the house.

"No, sir," called the sergeant. "Stand away from the house.''

Lazy little flames flickered at the open windows, gathered strength. In an hour, the fire *took* the house, became an angry inferno.

"Oh, Mama," Mattilda cried. She went to her mother and put her arms around her for comfort. But there was no comfort there. Her mother stood frozen as an icicle and watched her home falling into itself. Papa's face crumpled like a petulant baby's face. Mattilda couldn't bear it.

Grandpa Hume came to her, held her close and said, "Hold tight now.''

100

So she did, closed her eyes and talked to God, "If you're really all that good, help us now. Help us."

Although there was no apparent help from God, she calmed down and began looking for ways to fight. She picked up all the ripe corn she could and stuffed it into her apron pockets, hid several ears under a rock.

"What you doing, honey?" whispered Luella. "That little bit ain't going feed us."

"Saving seed."

Luella's face lit up. "Oh Lord, yes. Let me help." Then Luella felt the contradiction of what she doing, working against the Federals. "Well, *we* got to eat, ain't we?"

"Sure do," said Mattilda, working away and taking quick foxy looks at the nearest soldiers. She never once glanced back at the house, but the image of the six chimneys standing lonesome above the flaming ruins was indelible in her mind. Her tears blurred the golden corn tassels.

New orders snapped out, staccato and senseless, and she saw soldiers leading out the mule, Grandpa Hume's horse, finally Mulehead. There was no way to support this grief, no inner core of strength to help her. She could give up anything. Anybody. But not Mulehead. Mulehead was her little girl self, the connection between this dirty half-woman sweating in a cornfield and a happy untroubled little girl who never even heard the word Kanawha except as the name of a river and maybe an Indian. Mulehead had heard the secret fears and wishes that even Docia knew nothing about. Mulehead meant free days in the fields, fast gallops on the road.

She wished she had a gun. She would shoot the man leading Mulehead and Grandpa Hume's horse over to the fidgeting Yankee horses. She would shoot without fear or guilt.

The barn and outbuildings began burning.

At the same moment five horsemen rode in a line across the

winter garden, where kale, turnips, mustard greens, onions were well up in perfect well-tended rows, where bright pumpkins sat fat among dying vines. The horses began prancing, trampling the vegetables as if they were used to their work and enjoyed it. A pumpkin burst apart and stuck to a hoof.

And for the first time Abram spoke out. "No, sir, don't do that. No, mister."

Abram was not now a black man, nor a slave, nor a freed man. He was a *farmer* who had worked hard, and the destruction made the veins swell on his temples and his hands rise and curve as if they wanted to grab something and *kill* it.

The soldier nearest him was tall and limp, hunched over his horse like a rag. He gave Abram a negligent, unbothered look from under his ragged eyebrow and continued dancing his horse down the rows.

Abram looked wild, his laugh lines turned savage. He grabbed a hilling hoe, leaped toward the soldier, hoe held up. "No, sir, now. You stop!" he shouted.

Carelessly, unhurriedly, the tall soldier moved his gun around and fired. The blast caught Abram in mid-leap, lifted him higher. His scream was more in protest than pain. "Hey-y-y!" he yelled.

He fell to his hands and knees, crying, then crumpled downward, all his blood swiftly flowing out upon the earth he had defended.

Papa ran to Abram, tore off his shirt and tried to staunch the flow of blood, finally looked at Abram and gathered him to him, rocking him like a child. Abram never stirred. Papa's tears fell on him, and his mouth worked petulantly. Beside Mattilda, Luella sank to the ground weeping.

Mama stood frozen, an icy queen, her face deathly white. She stalked forward to the sergeant who held a hen, hypnotized and spiritless, under his arm.

"You have destroyed us. You have killed our friend. He

102

was a freed man. Weren't you supposed to be fighting *for* him? You have taken our food and houses.

"Yet my son died fighting on your side. My son-in-law was killed on his way to join your side. And until now, Sergeant, I have regarded myself as a Federal sympathizer. Are you satisfied with your day's work?"

The sergeant looked startled, and his eyes closed briefly. "Lady, I'm sorry. I hate it, doing this. But when you feed and shelter the Rebs, you kill *us*."

He looked down with embarrassment at the hen under his arm, and he stooped to release it, watched as it fluttered down and away with warning squawks.

"Leave us a horse to work the place," Mama said with cold hate. Not begging. Demanding. She pointed to Mulehead. He glanced at Mulehead, nodded, forked a thumb at a corporal who ran to Mulehead, brought him over and put the reins in her hands.

Mattilda felt relief, then swiftly guilt, because there was Abram dead in her father's arms, there was the house and barn and smokehouse and granary in ashes, the corn gone, the crops ruined.

The bluecoats now began to circle slowly out, getting wagons in line, heading south. South! Somebody must get warning to the salt works. For suddenly she had become a Confederate again.

Mattilda looked up the road toward Princeton. Still no sign of Michael's company.

Suddenly her fears, anguish, grief consolidated into fury. "Damn Yankees," she shouted. "Hey, damn Yankees. You forgot to burn the privies!"

Out of the long line of men on horses and in wagons, not a head turned, but in the last wagon, a soldier suddenly stooped and rolled two hams out upon the grass.

Thirty-five

December 1863

Mattilda had the knack of hammering the shingles into place better than her father did, and she moved swiftly across the sloped roof, row after row, while he puttered at the edge. "These don't match the main room," he complained.

"Doesn't matter, Papa."

The addition of the two log rooms to the schoolhouse, plus the kitchen behind the main room, had made the schoolhouse livable, although it now had a strange, unplanned look. Mattilda felt strong and competent, slipping the shingle into place and hitting the nail with two solid thuds. The neighbors had raised the two rooms, leaving them the shingling and the inside finishing to do (whenever, if ever, they could get some finishing boards). It was a big job because Bill struggled alone with the farming and Grandpa Hume had gone into a kind of palsy, which seemed not to touch his soul but kept surprising him because his hand would not do his will. It was up to Mattilda and Papa to do the shingling. She wished Docia could be there instead, they worked so perfectly in tandem.

"They *should* have put a chimney in *both* the rooms," her father complained. "How we going heat this building?"

Never this house, never our home. Papa regarded the schoolhouse as a homemade tent at the Wabash Campground, intended to be used for a few days and then forgotten. She truly believed he meant to rebuild New Place. Well, let that battle start when the time came. For now, get *this* home weatherproof and comfortable.

Mattilda had helped to add the rooms, and reasonable or not, she loved the schoolhouse in a way she hadn't loved the big house, although she sometimes awoke at night at the sound of Marjorie's baby crying or Elizabeth coughing, and she longed for her lost privacy.

Now, however, these bright, new, good-smelling shingles won her. She didn't mind that her dress was heavy with sweat and dirt or that her father was slow. The rhythm of her work, and the sounds—guinea squawks and pump handle squeaks, the December sun's heat on her shoulders, all gave her a feeling of well-being.

She heard someone on the ladder. "Docia? That you? Come on up. We do need you."

"I'm not Docia," a deep voice said, "but I'd be glad to help."

Mattilda jumped, tucked her skirts down. It was a very young man, not much older than herself, in a new, homemade, gray uniform. A handsome black-haired, red-bearded boy, with clear blue eyes and heavy black brows. He was familiar. But who?

"I'm Daniel Durham," he said, leaning against the roof. "I used to see you at camp meetings before the War."

"Oh, I know you. You're a blue-eyed Scot. Hello." Mattilda was acutely uncomfortable over her dirty dress. She probably smelled to heaven. He looked at the mass of work she'd done, at the long distance yet to go, looked embarrassed at catching her at a man's job.

After hello, what do you say? It wasn't like the olden days when you smiled and invited a young man into the parlor to meet your family, and then called for the help to bring refreshments.

She had known how to play her part all right, had watched all her sisters carefully. Now none of their lessons applied. He waited, pink-faced.

At least, she could be mannerly. She put her hammer aside and reached out a hand. "I never thought I'd be sitting on a roof, talking to Daniel Durham." He laughed and shook her hand warmly.

"Never pictured it myself, either. But it's important for me to be here, for I've brought you a present from your brother Joe."

"Joe? Where did you see him?"

"In Bland as they went through. Our county reserves fed his company, and he told me about your house being burned down. Sure was sorry. He said you all hadn't a piece of a mirror." From his blouse he hauled a small round mirror, beautifully framed with smooth dark wood, the handle fitting her hand as if she had been measured for it.

"Oh," Mattilda said. "Oh. Oh." It was a marvelous gift. She looked at herself, wiped a dirty line of sweat from her cheek, swept her hair back, felt confused at her pleasure and embarrassment.

"I look so terrible," she apologized, combing her hair with her fingers.

"Why, you don't." He watched, bemused.

"First time I've seen myself since the house burned, except in the water barrel."

"Be a shame not to see those pretty eyes," he said.

Why, he had come courting, she exulted. She wished she could holler and tell Mama.

"Thank you for thinking it," she said.

Then there was nothing to say again, but the silence was as comfortable as bees humming and birds twittering because she could tell from his quick, worried glances that he was thinking about how *he* looked to *her,* and that he paid no mind to her sweat and dirt.

"My father is on the other slope," she finally said. *Couldn't* say, "You are handsome, you have a good face, I like you." Besides he'd not know by the sound of work that Papa was there, huddled in a dream.

"Oh, then I'll go speak to him." He got up, walked sure-footed across the nail rows. Oh, he'd grown tall and good-looking. She listened to them talking, studied her mirror, tried to straighten her hair, scrubbed the sweat from her face and neck with her dress tail, smoothed her eyebrows, buttoned her top two buttons, resolved she'd not fidget. Waited. He was so long returning she began to think he'd gone down Papa's side of the house. There were many things she wished she had said. But presently he came back.

"You've still got a long way to go," he said, measuring the shingled part with his eyes.

"Yes." Then she felt she must explain why her side of the roof was half-done and the other side barely started. "The War has changed him."

Daniel nodded. Understood. "He was a good man. I remember him very well." She ducked to hide the sudden tears.

But she must let him know she was not accustomed to such work, that she was too womanly for this but only did it because she must.

"I reckon this is the worst roof shingling you ever saw." Laugh followed deprecated self.

He studied. "No, it ain't. It's one of the best. Done with art."

Oh, she liked this Daniel Durham. He was willing to let her be herself.

"If you want, I can help you till early evening," he said. "Be a long ride home and then up at daylight."

"What's happening at daylight?"

"My unit will hold drill. We may be assigned to the King's Salt Works."

A chill went over Mattilda. Better not to like him too well, her mind cautioned, or the War would take him away as it had Jason, Sarah, Michael, Bland Junior. Papa too, a sad voice added.

"I'm sorry to hear it," she said, taking up her hammer.

"I hate it myself," he agreed, without the excitement and militancy her brothers had exhibited. The glamour of war had settled into something ugly.

He began laying shingles ready to nail, and she saw that he had her father's hammer. "I told him to go down and rest, and I'd spell him awhile."

So they worked together through the afternoon. Mattilda looked at him occasionally to see if he was real, watched his big bony hands move with assurance, felt cared for, felt respected. Once he caught her looking, and they smiled. "Your daddy said it's all right for me to meet you all at the first camp meeting after the War. If you don't mind."

Oh, Mama, I've got an appointment with him, she wanted to sing over the roof edge.

"Why, that would be fine," she said, wondering if the blast of happiness had reddened her face.

"And I was wondering if you'd care to correspond."

She nodded wordlessly. Now he would know about her hen-scratching, but he'd not judge her for it, she felt sure.

He wrote his name and address on a bit of paper in careful, perfect little letters, not at all the way those great hands might have scrawled. She studied the paper, and it immediately became personal and dear to her. *This* was the way he wrote.

They nearly finished their work, yet Daniel left the roof with regret. "I wish I had three more hours," he said.

108

"Never mind. You've done enough that I can easily do the rest."

He let her go down the ladder alone, respectful of her independence, and he followed, said his good-byes to the family. "Don't wait for me to write first," he urged her quietly. "I'll write first chance, and you do the same."

She nodded, and he mounted his horse and left.

Without a word to the teasing faces of her family, she ran to the privy. Relieved, she sat and dreamed.

She suddenly laughed aloud. She bet Daniel had ridden just out of sight and had run for the woods. Maybe some day, she would know him well enough to ask.

Thirty-six

January 1864

Mattilda accepted the fact that men killed each other in a war, the women died in childbirth, that grandfathers died of old age (Not Grandpa Hume—he *had* to be immortal), but she began to question whether God really was in charge of things when Marjorie's baby girl arrived two months early and began to slip away from them.

The birth was easy and swift. Yet Mama in great anxiety brought the naked unwashed baby to the main room.

"Open the window, Matt." She held the little body upside down, her fingers looped strongly around its ankles. The baby hung, a dead weight, unmoving. Boldly her mother slapped its buttocks once, twice, finally three times and the cry came, pitiful and mewling, without strength, but enough to get the breathing going.

Her mother looked grim. "Afraid we're not going to keep you, little missy." She held the baby to her for a moment, kissed the cheek where a curving line of drying blood clung, handed her to Mattilda.

"Afterbirth hasn't come, so I need to help Marjorie," she said. "You and Docia have to try to save this baby."

The baby had a perfect shape, a plump doll baby, but deep blue blotches covered most of her body, and she was tinier than any human being Mattilda had ever seen before. She struggled and cried feebly. Mattilda stared with fascination at the tied-off cord, big as the baby's wrist.

"Now, Matt, it's up to you. Get Docia. Build the fire up and get her warm as you can. Surround her with heat. Use hot bricks in towels and the stone water heater. Careful, don't burn her." The crisp orders snapped out.

"I have to get back to Marjorie." At the door Dorothy Repass turned. "MATTILDA! Get at it. Holler for Docia." She paused. "The baby hasn't much chance to live, honey."

Preparing her, Mattilda suddenly realized. She came out of her shock, grabbed up a folded quilt and wrapped up the baby, yelled through the open window, "Docia! Get in here quick!" Slammed the window. Examined the tiny face. Eyes tight closed against the world. Deep breath, small cry prolonged, tremor.

Docia arrived. "Poor little soul," she said expertly. "She be dead before long."

"She will not!" Mattilda screamed. "Hurry now. Get the stone heater full of hot water first. Then get bricks, heat them in the oven."

As she talked, she worked with savage haste, built the fire so big it endangered the chimney and the house.

Docia came with the jug and a cup of warm sugar water with a baby spoon. Left at once to heat the bricks.

Deep breath, long cry, tremor. The baby clutched Mattilda's finger and worked at living. Oh, honey baby, try hard.

It was still not warm enough. Mattilda quickly shed her dress, threw it aside, stripped her underwear down to the waist, held the naked baby against her own hot skin, wrapped the quilt around them both, sat Indian fashion on the bed, waiting. The sweetness of the baby was overwhelming.

She began an argument with God. "If you will let her live, I'll forgive you for the War."

She waited and listened. Implosion of breath, cry, tremor. Her own body began steaming and she held the little girl close. In a few minutes the crying stopped and she couldn't feel the breathing though her nerves stretched taut to know, but the baby felt warm and alive, so she sat still and waited.

"This is a good time to stop the dwindling," she told God and she tried to ignore the terrible silence.

Docia came in, saw the dress, looked at her strangely. "I got the hot bricks. Let's fix her cradle in a basket, put her close to the fire."

"Not yet. Let her sleep awhile, get her some strength first."

Mattilda's whole self surrounded and cradled the baby. She would be a womb to comfort her.

Docia sat on the bed. "You sure she's all right?"

"Yes. Getting her first nap."

Silence was not part of Docia's nature, and she talked about her future, about studying to be a teacher of black children. She would help them get a *good* start. Mattilda's ears heard, but her mind clung to the small, warm, unmoving body.

"Can she breathe all right?"

"Certainly. I have an air hole down to her face." She thrust her left hand up from the quilt in demonstration.

111

"She hasn't cried once," Docia suggested, her concerned eyes not wavering from Mattilda's face.

She's worried about *me,* Mattilda realized. Thinks I'm crazy.

"This baby is not dead, Docia. She's asleep. She's warm as toast."

Docia suddenly left the room, and Mattilda was glad. But immediately Mama was there, Docia with her, watchful and ready as a catbird.

"Could the baby be dead, honey?" her mother asked. Right to the point. No hemming and hawing.

"No, ma'am," said Mattilda emphatically. "She's warm, and she feels alive."

But terror began to take Mattilda's mind as it had in the days after Jason died. I'll never forgive you, God.

"Is she moving?"

"No."

"Let me have her then. Marjorie is ready for her. Maybe she can nurse a little."

Mattilda had to fight her reluctance. This was Marjorie's baby, not hers. But worse, would the baby move? She was afraid to find out. She swung her feet to the floor, unfolded the quilt, felt her way to the baby, lifted her in the quilt. Felt a violent jump of fear, heard the cry again, louder and stronger.

Docia and Mama slumped with relief and laughed aloud. "Whoooeeeee," said Docia.

Body-naked to the waist, not noticing or caring, Mattilda took the little girl to Marjorie.

The dwindling had slowed, maybe even stopped.

"I forgive you," she told the ceiling.

She must write a letter to Daniel tonight. Good news, she would say. Marjorie's baby girl came early, and I helped keep her alive.

112

Thirty-seven

July 1864

Dorothy Repass never argued with Bland Senior any more, no matter how aggravating he became. He ranted and gesticulated; she murmured soothing responses. The walk to church was always like this now.

Eager to get into church and out of the drifting mist, Mattilda and Docia walked ahead of the rest, then her parents, then Grandpa Hume and Elizabeth trailing. Luella was at home, needing rest more than religion and Marjorie stayed with the baby.

As usual when she left home, Mattilda felt that a long string held her, stretching longer and thinner with every step, never quite snapping apart so that she could forget what she'd left. The string that held her today was the thought of the baby—Annie—who was too sweet to leave alone for a minute. She kept remembering the feel of Annie's small self cradled close in her arms. So wee, so full of curiosity, so surprised when her own leg suddenly kicked, so hurt and angry if attention was not immediately forthcoming. Mattilda could never get enough of looking at her.

She and Docia walked in silence, thinking their separate thoughts. Docia seemed morose, unlike her usual lively self.

Behind them Papa's voice grew louder.

"We'll whip them. You wait. We've got them running now!" He sounded angry. Mama did not respond.

Mattilda glanced back. One side of her father's face was drawn and one eye bulged a little, staring blindly. One arm chopped the air with every word and the other arm hung unmoving. He limped, looked like the ghost of her father, still wearing his best suit which now hung in folds. Mattilda suddenly pictured her loom and the beautiful cloth she had made for his next suit. Before the fire. There had never been time to make it up into a suit. She sighed. When would they ever get another loom?

It was a long walk to church from where they lived now. Used to be that she *wanted* to walk (when the distance was short), and Mama would say, "No, we'll ride together as a family." But now with only old Mulehead to pull and nothing but an open wagon used for carrying manure and grain, it seemed more dignified to walk.

Now they passed the old house, chimneys still standing guard over the desolation, a rich growth of vine mercifully hiding the worst of the black scars.

There was the hydrangea bush they'd brought from Grandma Hume's house when Mattilda was born. Tomorrow for sure she would bring it home in the wheelbarrow and set it out.

"They were smart all right!" Her father suddenly shouted. "They knew where to come."

Mattilda looked back. Papa stood in the middle of the road, pointed to the ruins.

"Yes," agreed Mama smoothly. "They knew *when* to come too. Hit right at corn harvest. Made me wonder if they hadn't known all the time what we planned. Maybe even watched through a telescope from the mountains." She took her husband's arm to coax him past the ruins. He jerked away.

114

"Corn harvest!" he said petulantly. "Corn didn't matter to them. It was maps they wanted. They were after my war maps. Burned my maps, damn them." He hacked away with his left hand.

Mattilda turned away, sick. Oh, little Papa.

"Ain't that right, Grandpa Hume? Wasn't it the maps?" he roared.

"That's true, Bland Senior. Maps are important." Grandpa Hume said.

Appeased, her father walked on.

Relief. Argument averted. Quiet conversations started up again.

"Docia, you haven't said word one. What you thinking?"

"Thinking about church."

"What about it?"

Docia gave Mattilda a searching look. "I do believe, Matt, your head is so in the clouds over Daniel Durham that you don't notice what's in front of your nose."

It was true, and she didn't try to deny it. "What about the church?"

"A feeling I get in church. Feels to me like the white people beginning to blame us colored people for the War. You ain't noticed that? We being separated off. You surely been seeing it."

Mattilda shook her head in bafflement. "No, truly. I haven't noticed anything."

"Surely, you've seen black faces in back of church, white in front."

"Mattilda, looks like you could walk with your own family to church," Bland Senior suddenly roared.

Mattilda started, looked at Docia who hunched her shoulders and grimaced slightly, signalling a silent *See what I'm saying?*

115

"Come on. Let's drop back so he'll hush," Mattilda urged. Help me keep the peace, she meant.

But Docia's eye turned downward in a way she had lately of hiding her thoughts. She shook her head, walked faster, separated herself entirely from the straggling group. Mattilda waited for her parents to catch up. She tried to keep from feeling anything, tried to think, Well, there goes Docia ahead of me, wants to get to church first. Tried to remain untouched. Docia, my friend. Couldn't withstand the slow anguish building in her breast, couldn't hold back the tears that would reveal her hurt to her mother's quick eyes. She walked the rest of the way slightly in front of her father who at last seemed satisfied to be still.

In church, she looked quickly around. First impression: scattered fans moving with steady rhythm. Second impression: back rows filled with blacks, rest of the church with scattered whites.

Docia sat alone on the fourth row from the back, the rest of the bench empty. She didn't look up as the Repasses came in. Mattilda hesitated. Knew she should proceed to the front right where her family always sat. Stopped by Docia's bench and stood till her parents had passed her. Still stood till Elizabeth and Grandpa Hume caught up, glanced at her speculatively, passed. Still stood, though all conversations had ceased in the church, and now there were only the sounds of swishing fans and the happy gurgling cry of a baby.

Still stood when she became aware of a definite feeling of fear growing in the blacks, the hope she wouldn't start anything. Docia looked up in fright, and Mama looked back, anxiety plain on her face.

It was not right.

Still stood when Papa got up and turned to her, pointed a finger. "Get up here with your family."

116

Now the fans stopped.

It was not right. *Old* Bland Senior would *never* have said that. *Old* Bland Senior was her father, not this poor rambling, dwindling man.

Without a word she went into the row and sat by Docia.

Her decision did not lessen her anguish, because she felt now that she and her family were miles apart.

"Mattilda!" Papa said.

Then Mama got up, pulled at him. "Let her *be*. Hear me? Let her be." He grumbled, wavered, whispered to himself, and sat down.

Grandpa Hume looked back, smiled and touched two fingers to his eyebrow in salute. Slowly her pain and fright faded as she and Docia sang together from the hymnal.

Daniel Durham, how would *you* see it? she thought. Would you understand why I should sit by my friend even in times when people made it seem wrong?

She truly hoped so because no matter how he saw it, she must do what *she* knew was right, just as Sarah had done. Her sudden memory of Sarah gave her support and conviction she had lacked, gave her ease.

Thirty-eight

October 1864

King's Salt Works
October 5, 1864

Dear Miss Repass,

My visit with you on your rooftop seems now like a happy dream in the distant past. I can barely believe it happened, but I hold to the memory as well as I can.

Much has happened to me in recent days. General Burbridge came at us with thousands of men, up from Kentucky and aiming to break the railroad and to ruin the saltworks. I was running ahead of them trying to catch up with my company and will confess my fright nearly laid me out. Colonel Giltner's cavalry kept the Yankees busy till the Reserves were in position. We got the brunt of it on Oct. 2nd at Saunders' place, which I would like to show you sometime. I can't believe it was only two days ago. Old men and boys is what they *used* to call us. We were hurt bad, several killed, and were pushed back, but we held on till help came. And then Burbridge got pushed away. Last we knew, Col. Giltner was still chasing him.

War is even worse than I thought. It would break your heart to hear men crying and to see them die. And that's all I'll say about the terrible part. (*What about you, Daniel? Oh my good friend, be careful.*)

I came through it untouched except for a bruise covering the whole left side of my cheek and I can't remember how I got it. Thank the Lord for his mercy to me.

(*And a devout* AMEN!)

I met a friend of your family, older fellow, a Mr. Ray Beard. Said he'd been off fighting in the South and hadn't seen any of you since the beginning of the War. Told him your family news and I also told him you were a little beauty. And he said Oh is that so? Maybe I'll call on the family if I get back there. (*Head swimming. Sickness. Daniel delivering her into the hands of the enemy.*)

Mr. Beard is a grain trader now and is trying to feed our troops.

(*Grain stealer, more like.*)

I told him I had firm intentions toward you and not to go behind my back and sweet-talk you.

(*Firm intentions! Mama had better not read this letter, though if you come to it, she* was *going on sixteen and plenty of girls had beaus by then.*)

May the Lord take care of you and your loved ones.

Most respectfully,

X ---

Daniel Durham

P.S. The Federals had a negro cavalry regiment and they fought bravely. They were not like the negros I have known who would *never* have ridden into danger that way, like they were glued to their horses' backs.

(*Lucas would have.* Abram *would have.* Docia *would have! And what's more Docia would teach you to capitalize Negro.*)

P.S. My mother will soon send you an invitation to visit our home during Christmas and I have already put in for a furlough from Dec. 20 to Dec. 26, giving me a day to ride up there and a day to ride back, with five wonderful days of making your closer acquaintance. You do please stay on long enough to get to know my family better. You know, our parents have been friends for years and it's time their children became friends.

(Mama would never let her go. You're too young for that, she'd say.)

Thirty-nine

Writing letters to a man was hard to do. You wanted to sound as grown-up as possible, yet able to explain the tight hold your mother kept on you, without seeming to mind it. How to start.

Mattilda read Daniel's letters, read them, read them, till his handwriting and words were memorized and still she couldn't get enough. Now she unfolded them once more and read them. Her memory of him was patchy though sudden recollections sometimes brought him flickering back and gave her heart a nudge. But the *letters* had become Daniel. He explained and expostulated about the War, felt heroic and afraid by turns, and confessed all to her.

She liked him for it, and she longed to see him; she thought about him all day, every day. Without her intentions, her mind busied itself constantly with the singing words, phrases, thoughts she would put into her next letter to him. Now that she sat with pen and paper, ready to write, the flowing lovely words evaporated and left her with simple wooden sentences that were bound to show him what a country girl she was.

Besides, she must be cheerful, no matter what, because the burdens of a fighting soldier were enough without her adding to them.

Dear Mr. Durham,

(My dear friend Daniel)

It would indeed be a comfort to me to receive word that you are in excellent spirits and health.

(I hope you still have no wounds. I hope you are not afraid, as I am, all the time.)

My family is in excellent health and sends warm greetings to you.

(Papa is lost in this world. Mama has turned snappish and I understand and wish I could wipe away her worries.)

Grandpa Hume moved back to his old home where he will be more comfortable with his own bedroom. My aunt will give him good care. *(Grandpa Hume couldn't live like this, cramped up in three little rooms. But I've lost my best friend except for Docia and maybe you. Grandpa Hume's hand shakes all the time, and he spills things but we laugh together and he makes me brave. How will I face the next terrors without him? I miss him. Mama frets about him and says, I do hope Ellie will see to it that he eats.)*

I caution you again about Ray Beard in case he ever returns to your camp. We are very sure he and other renegades killed Jason, but they escaped justice by entering the Confederate army down South, and now I suppose they are regarded as heroes. He is the first one with nerve enough to come back to Virginia.

(I'll never forgive Ray Beard. I'll hate him till the day I die. And I'm afraid of him. What man is there to protect this house from him if he comes back?)

Some Confederate veterans are home again, wounded or

sick, and they have come calling on my family. They have been shocked and sympathetic to see how we live now.

(Don't think, Daniel Durham, that you're the only man in my world. In case you decide you don't like me, there are others.)

I was sorry to read that your food supplies are so low. Maybe by now you have been able to forage for more. What does that mean, forage for food? I trust the Lord will keep you safe.

We are worried about my brother Joe back in his old company near Winchester. They say there are five Federals for every Confederate there. But who can believe rumors? Both Runyon boys are dead and the fights get fiercer all the time. *(Mama is sick with worry.)*

We pray for Joe every night. *(I pray for you.)*

My kindest regards,

(I think I love you. Even Docia will not tease me about you because I can't keep the tears away. I love you, I'm pretty sure.)

Mattilda Repass (Mattie)

P.S. No use to keep back the bad news, because you will hear it sooner or later. Bill left with our Reserves to defend Richmond. *(Papa never even noticed.)*

Forty

Daniel's arrival was as much a surprise to Mattilda as his first visit. He showed up suddenly at the front door, embarrassing

122

Mattilda who now must invite him into the kitchen-living-dining room and let him see for himself that they lived like savages.

She had been churning with furious speed—get it over with and get to something more interesting—when she heard heavy feet on the doorstep. Who? Grandpa Hume? Bill coming back from the War? A neighbor? She opened the door, stared at Daniel, got caught again by his blue eyes, laughed to see his fist still upheld ready to knock and his mouth hanging open.

"Daniel! Mr. Durham!" This time she had sense to hold out her hand right away and he took it, stood there like an idiot, nodding and grinning wordlessly. He looked tired and dusty. His hand was bigger than she remembered, hard as wood. Oh, he was big. Oh, good-looking.

She got him through the door and said to her mother who stood at the stove and to Marjorie (holding the baby) and to Elizabeth (sewing at the table), "Mama, sisters, here's Daniel Durham." Pleading silently, Don't tease us. Respect him.

Still he'd not said a word.

"Why, Daniel. I'm so *proud* to see you. Come sit down," Mama said, indicating the three rockers at the right side of the room, and holding out her hand, for all the world as much at ease as she used to be in the parlor.

At last he found his tongue, realized he still held Mattilda's hand, released it and shook hands with her mother.

"Why, ma'am, thank you. I had a chance to drop by, had to come to Burke's Garden on an official errand anyway and thought I'd run by and check on you folks." Quick look of apology at Mattilda.

Burke's Garden! Don't anybody laugh. Please. Burke's Garden was a good thirty miles of mountain riding. He had ridden an extra day.

"Stop by to see your family, did you?" Mama asked, heading him toward the chairs.

"Well, no, ma'am, there wasn't enough time." Shy look at Mattilda. He had passed up the chance to see his family to come here!

He nodded to Marjorie and Elizabeth, smiled at the baby. "How you ladies feeling?" Smiles, nods all around.

"Fine, Daniel. Except for the everlasting War, you know."

He had *yet* to say a single word to Mattilda.

"No, I shouldn't sit on your good furniture." Mattilda looked in silence at the homemade split oak chairs, thought for a second of the elegant polished chairs she used to take for granted. "Let me go out and smack off some of this dust and rinse my face and hands." He reached over to drop his cap on a chair post.

"You do that. We're fixing to eat in a little while. Cornbread and leatherbritches." No apologies for the fare.

"That sounds good. And then I've got to get started back."

Still not a word to her and leaving right away.

"Mama," Mattilda said desperately. "I'll get Daniel to help me get the water."

"No need, Mattilda. He doesn't want to do that. We can manage the water."

"Oh, no, ma'am," urged Daniel. "I want to help."

There was no well at their new house, but the spring was cool and dark, surrounded by fern, violets and heartleaves, shaded by hardwoods. A place dear to Mattilda during her school days and the only place nearby where she could be private and quiet for a few minutes.

He would *have* to talk to her there. But Newt Jackson was at the spring resting on his way home. Darn his skin, he *never* stopped there. Why today? She introduced him to Daniel and while they filled the buckets, the two men talked about the battle over the saltworks and what it was like now down around Marion and Saltville and so on till she was ready to scream with rage.

Not a word to her yet.

His blue eyes looked at her more and more frequently, answering Newt Jackson's questions to her as if *she*'d asked them.

After a bit Daniel became silent, then groped in a pocket for something, silently handed it to her. It was a candy heart with a message. *Will you marry me?* it said.

Marry him? Was it a bad joke? She studied his face, and he looked ready to cry.

"Now you take the Confederate soldier," said Newt Jackson, sitting back against the rocks. "He's a soldier that can do without no new clothes or weapons and without hardly no food and yet out-ride and out-walk and out-shoot the enemy. Like he don't need much."

"Some day?" Daniel said aloud, his first words to her.

"What do you mean—*some* day?" Newt Jackson snorted. "Any day. They can out-do the Northern soldier any day of the week and Sunday, too."

Mattilda kept studying Daniel's red face. He was serious. She nodded and they stood apart, smiling.

In a moment, Daniel picked up the big buckets. "You're wrong, Mr. Jackson. Southern soldier gets just as hungry as the Northern one, and he can't shoot a bullet if he ain't got one."

Take that and smoke it in your pipe, you talky old fool, Mattilda thought happily.

On the path toward the house, they talked with urgent speed.

"I won't be sixteen till April."

"It's all right. We'll wait till the war is over and they let us.

125

I'm just seventeen myself. Maybe time you're seventeen, you think?''

She didn't know. All she knew was a singing happiness as Daniel told her of the land his father had given him at Bear Creek. ''Bear Creek? Where's that?'' He thumbed west.

''We'd have to grub-farm. It's way up on the mountain, you know.''

He talked and talked and talked, more than the talky old fool they'd left at the spring, and still she was not weary of listening.

Forty-one

Mattilda was afraid to bring the subject up, knew in advance the pain it would give her mother. Yet she had kept silent now for so many years that her own pain was ready to burst forth like angry corruption.

''Mama, after the War, will families get back together?''

Her mother put her Bible on the table, pushed her eyeglasses to the top of her head, gazed bleakly at Mattilda. ''I don't know.''

''But what happened in other wars?''

''I don't know. I wish I had a book to read about it. All I know is that a great-uncle on my mother's side was a loyalist in Revolutionary times and he went back to England and the family never heard from him again.''

''Oh *no*,'' whispered Mattilda. Caving in of courage. Pain out of control. She and her mother looked at each other, tied together by a strong rope of helpless agony.

Three and a half years since they'd seen her.

"I write to her once a month," Mama said. "But never a word from her. Not *directly* from her."

Mattilda picked up her pen. She considered a moment. She mustn't mention Ray Beard. Sarah could never forgive the South for letting him go free. Mattilda couldn't either, but Sarah might not believe that.

October 19, 1864

Dear Sarah,

Since I last saw you, I have grown up. I have a beau, Daniel Durham of the reserve defenders at Saltville, and *he* thinks I am beautiful. What do you think of that?

I want to keep this letter light-hearted, the way we used to be. I guess Mama wrote you the Federals burnt our house and we now live in the schoolhouse, and right near where you used to stand to teach Latin, there is now a door to the bedroom where Marjorie and the baby and I sleep. Elizabeth sleeps on a cot where the blackboard and map were and what was the front door is now a door to Papa and Mama's bedroom. Do you picture how cozy we are?

We have plans for another room in the back (what used to be the *side* where I sat), and this room will be for you and Elizabeth and little Jason when you come home.

That's what I'm really writing about, Sarah. About you coming home. Please come. Please come. Please.

You are always in our prayers.

Your loving sister,
Mattie

P.S. Sarah, the War is not the fault of anyone here. We are all women except for Papa, and the War has killed him as surely as it did Jason and Michael and Bland Junior. Right now he is up at the old place pushing the ashes about with his cane and looking for his maps. This is his *work,* and he does it every day. When he finds his maps, he says, he will build a wall to tack the maps onto and he will use that wall for the beginning of the new big house. Papa can't understand that the schoolhouse is the way we live now.

But even if the War *were* our fault, couldn't you find it in your heart to forgive us and come home?

I do beg your pardon for not keeping this letter light-hearted as I promised.

M.R.

She carried the letter to the mill, thinking as she walked that she would not allow herself to watch for a reply. She would busy herself with other thoughts so that the wait would seem short.

For surely, *surely* Sarah would respond.

Forty-two

"Mama, don't worry. I'm wounded but not dying," Joe's letter went. "But Cedar Creek ended the War for me. Is there any able-bodied man there who can bring a wagon for me? The lieutenant says he will see that I get to New Market Gap, and I will stay with the Hawkinses till you send for me. I hate to burden you, Mama, but the field hospital is out of commission now, and I can't get the needed nursing. I still can't walk."

The words burned into their minds. The idea of having even

one horse or one buggy was preposterous although Joe couldn't know that. And there were *no* able-bodied men for the long, *long* journey. Mama and Elizabeth would have to go, once they had a team and wagon.

Mama and Mattilda grimly hitched Mulehead to their rickety wagon and went to the mill to trade for horses and a wagon.

"What we going to trade, Mama?" Mattilda asked.

"Only one thing we got," her mother said. "Land."

"Oh, Mama." But think as she could, Mattilda couldn't come up with anything else. It would be Newt Jackson they would trade with then, for he had teased them as long as Mattilda could remember for the northeast section which bordered on his own little farm. Surely Mama would not let the bottom go for a wagon and a team. She studied her mother's face for a moment, dared not interrupt the sad inward-turned look which meant that Mama was resolving her problems with the best bargain she could come up with.

Newt Jackson sat on the mill porch waiting as if he expected them. "I need to borrow your good team and wagon," Mama said, not waiting to discuss the weather or War or the rye failure. She was going at it wrong, Mattilda realized, too eager to get the horses and go.

"Going for Joe, are ye?" Newt asked, eying her mother with a knowing, sidelong look. He had read the letter before it was passed on to them.

Mattilda had a frail last hope that her mother would duck the question, would not let him know their desperate need lest the bargaining be completely one-sided. But her staunch honesty could not waver even at such a time.

"Yes."

"Well now." Newt Jackson hugged himself, scratched his back as far as he could reach. "They're still fighting there, ain't they? I hear tell the Confederates are grouping at New Market and you'd have to go right through there." (No hint that she planned to go *exactly* there, Mattilda thought with fury. As if he had not read the letter.)

He shook his head. "Be too risky to *loan* the team. You know. Might get killed. Or might get took by either side."

"Then I'd like to buy," her mother said calmly.

"Offering Confederate money?" he asked, ready to say no.

"Newt, trade with me honestly. You know all we got is land."

He grimaced. It wasn't mannerly to go to the heart of the bargain without preliminary rituals.

"Land ain't worth nothing now."

"Bottom land is always worth something."

His eyes gleamed. So it had come to it.

"Which piece?"

"I'm offering that field from the sycamore other side of the church back to the beech grove."

It was their best land. Over a hundred acres.

"And the land from the church back to the other side of the cemetery hill to the three chestnut oaks?" he suggested, giving an accurate description of their deed. Twenty more acres. It would gut the farm.

Dorothy Repass chewed her lower lip, looked blankly past him. "That land has been in my husband's family for sixty years." He shrugged.

Not another decent team in fifty miles, Mattilda thought with hatred.

"I'll need a gun to take and a gun to leave, plus ammunition," she countered. He nodded. "I'll need feed for the horses and grain for bargaining along the way." He continued his slow nodding. "We keep cemetery rights and road rights to it." Still nodding.

Mattilda had begun crying, could not keep it back. Her mind worried with the only cussword she could think of— Devil, Devil, Devil, Devil—because that's what Newt Jackson turned out to be. Her mother's hand clasped her arm firmly. "Mattilda." Her tears dried up.

"Mama, we aren't horse traders. We need a sworn promise these horses will last the whole trip," Mattilda urged.

"Last? Hell, Mattilda, excuse me, these horses could start at the bottom of this country and go to the top, then across and down and back again and rest a week and do it again."

"Then it's a guarantee?" her mother asked.

"Well, they could cast a shoe and you surely couldn't blame *that* on me."

"Throw in shoes and nails then," Mama said. "We'll find a smithy if we need one."

"All right." He shook his head irritably.

"It's a guarantee now?" Mattilda pressed him.

"Y'all feed them, water them but don't bloat them, rest them, don't let them get shot or get they legs broke, it's a guarantee."

"Write it in the bargain, Mama."

"Write it? Y'all don't trust me to sell you good horses?" he protested. "We don't have to write it down."

"We can get to Princeton all right," Mattilda said. "Mr. Johnston up in Princeton has begged Papa for years to sell him that field."

"All right now. All right. Write in the guarantee that if the horses don't make it back, you'll pay for them later in grain or silver." He thrust a sudden scolding finger. "If they do make it back, the land is mine. Dorothy Repass, don't you let those horses die on purpose."

"Give me some paper and I'll write it up," Mama said. "We'll get the deed made when I get back."

131

"How about Bland Senior? He going to sign?" Newt asked cautiously.

"He'll sign."

After Newt Jackson went for the horses, Mattilda asked, "How *will* you get him to sign, Mama?"

Her mother's face crumpled. "I have to lie to him. I'll tell him I'm bargaining to get his maps back."

They started home, Mattilda with the new team, her mother trying to coax Mulehead into moving.

"One-sided kiss, Mama," Mattilda called out. Her mother smacked her lips and Mulehead started obediently.

Newt Jackson had done a good job of stowing the grain and feed forward in the wagon so that packing the food and clothes and bedding for Mama and Elizabeth was quickly accomplished, plus wrapping the loaded gun and hiding it under the seat. They took the only tarpaulin on the farm, for the wagon had no kind of cover and Joe would need protection against the cold fall rain, maybe even sleet at the mountain passes.

Her mother wrote the description of the trip down for Marjorie and Mattilda. "Just in case," she said.

In case what? Mattilda wondered. What could they do about it in case something happened? Still she felt better holding a bit of paper.

"To Princeton to Narrows to Shannons (for the night) to Peppers Ferry across New River to Christiansburg to Salem to Lexington to Kerrs' Creek (to stay at the Kerrs' home for a rest), to the Staunton Kerrs to Harrisonburg to New Market (to rest with the Hawkinses and get Joe) and home the same route."

They would camp out any night they could not reach a friend's home. Mattilda had made this trip when she was small, much of it on the train, a rough hard trip even with that luxurious way of travel. But with the railroad bridges out all the way to Wytheville, the risk was too great that swift-moving Federals would attack the rest of the line, maybe even the trains themselves.

And Joe couldn't *walk* yet. He needed to lie down. *Why* couldn't he walk? Too weak? Or his legs, could it be that? She turned from the thought as she had a hundred times, as she knew her mother and sisters had too.

Papa was not there to say good-bye, was at the old place on his everlasting search in the ashes.

"Girls, watch out for your father," Mama pleaded. "He'll likely wonder what's happening."

"We'll watch him, Mama," Marjorie promised.

"Tell him every day I'm on the way home."

"We will."

They left at last. Elizabeth, beautiful as ever, took the reins, both women dignified in their best dresses and bonnets as if they were going to church. Mattilda stood with Marjorie, small Annie straddling her hip, and they waved and waved till at last the wagon rounded the brushy curve and the fluttering hands disappeared.

"Comes somebody," Marjorie said, looking down the opposite direction toward the mill. "Looks like we'll have company for dinner."

The man came at a good clip, leaning forward eagerly. His horse looked sassy and well-fed.

Both women studied the approaching horseman, couldn't make out who it was.

"God help us," Mattilda said suddenly. "It's Ray Beard." She felt the blood drop from her face, felt dizzy and sick, saw Jason turning slowly toward her holding out a paper that said TRAITOR.

"What on *earth?*" Marjorie cried angrily. "He can just turn himself around and *git.*"

But Ray Beard, with no apparent sensitivity to their feelings, dismounted with stolid self-assurance, stood holding his hat and smiling.

"Let's see," he said, "You're Miss Marjorie. Couldn't forget *you*. But then the quick jaw thrust dismissed her and he turned to Mattilda.

"My God, you *are* a beauty. Heard you were but didn't hear it strong enough."

Mattilda felt sick and dirty, the old dwindling taking hold and shriveling her spirit.

"Ray Beard, get on that horse and get out of this yard," Marjorie said, snappish as a water turtle. "You'll never be welcome at the Repass house."

"Why?" he asked in honest amazement. "Because I helped hang a Yankee enemy?"

No hesitation about admitting it now.

"Get off our land," Marjorie said.

"Say you so too, Miss Mattilda?"

Mattilda could not speak through her choking hate and fear. She drew back her arm and waved him away in a gesture of revulsion. He shrugged, remounted, sat there in no hurry to leave and looked at the house and brambly fields.

"You ain't what you was," he said.

"Yes, we are," said Mattilda, "and you're what *you* were too." It was a good hit like a cussword.

"When the War is over," Marjorie said, "and when law is re-established, we will file a claim against you again and have you tried for murder."

He shrugged, grinned. "That day will never come. Nobody's going to hang me for killing the enemy."

He ignored Marjorie. "Good-bye, Miss Mattilda, till I see you again."

134

"Never," she said. "Never."

His eyes traveled down her dress, lingered. Then he rode back toward the mill.

Mattilda's heart-pounding began to slow and she tried to control her sick fear. Oh, if Sarah were only here. Or Grandpa Hume.

At that moment, Docia stepped out from behind the house. She held Luella's only kitchen knife, long, slim, handmade. "If that sajer had tried anything, I was fixing to stab him to bloody bits," she said cheerfully.

Mattilda felt better at once and the three women laughed shakily as they entered the house.

"Eat with us, Docia," Mattilda begged. "I never get to see you any more."

"All right. It's my birthday and it'll be like a celebration."

"Oh, I've got a gift for you," Mattilda said. She got a little book, the only one she owned, the only one saved from the fire. On the fly leaf was written "Mattilda Repass. Presented by New Place S. S. Sept. 26th, 1858."

Docia read and smiled, turned to the title:

THE GARDEN OF THE LORD:
or, Sanctification
Both
Progressive and Instantaneous.

The gift was a success, Mattilda realized. Although she had tried a hundred times to read the book, she had always given in and turned to something else to do. But Docia would read it.

"It's my first book," Docia said. "It'll help me be a teacher."

As they ate, their talk drifted comfortably, and slowly Mattilda's fear subsided till at last she could think of her mother urging the horses along on the long dangerous journey.

135

Forty-three

November 1864

It was a cold fall day before they got back, and only bits of color lingered in the trees. Newt Jackson unintentionally warned them that the wagon was on the way from Princeton when he raced his horse by like lightning streaking up the pike.

"They're coming," Marjorie said. "There goes old Newt."

Mattilda grabbed her father's heavy coat and swung into it, ran up the road after Newt Jackson. Be quicker to go on my own than try to encourage Mulehead to hurry, she thought. From the crest of the church hill she saw the wagon coming, slowly, slowly, pulling to the left, then back. Newt's horse cantered around and around it, and he gesticulated furiously.

Mattilda stopped, gasping for air and waited for the stitch in her side to settle. She couldn't see Joe, but from this distance, her mother and Elizabeth sat on the seat looking exactly as they had a month ago. They were not yet on Repass property. She walked swiftly to meet them, and as she came close, she saw the reason for Newt's agitation. One horse moved a step or two, hesitated and shuddered. The second horse walked with good strength, pulling the whole load, but stopping to wait for his sick partner.

"Mama! Elizabeth!" Mattilda shrieked. "Where's Joe?"

"Hey, little sister," she heard him call, and a hand waved from the side of the wagon bed. "I'm here."

She avoided Newt Jackson's high-stepping horse and ran around back of the wagon, looked at Joe. Couldn't believe it *was* Joe, this sick, skinny ghost, his tawny hair as dark as Michael's used to be. Wrapped in quilts, he sat half-upright, propped against the seat back.

"Why, you pretty thing," he said, reaching a hand. She couldn't reach him, started to climb aboard.

"Lay off, Mattilda," her mother said sharply.

Hurt, she drew back. "I want to kiss my brother hello," she said.

"Mama wants to be fair. She won't add an ounce of extra weight," Joe said. He grinned, showing a gap where his top teeth had been. Shock. Yet she almost saw the old Joe again.

"Oh." Mattilda took a step or two to catch up with the barely moving wagon.

"Stay away, Mattilda," Newt Jackson shouted. "No fair to git on." His horse trotted briskly around again. "Where's the property line? Ain't we on your property yet?"

"The bargain says to the *house*," Mama said.

"That horse ain't going to make it to the house," Mattilda said.

"It's what I told Mama," Joe cackled, full of glee like an old man.

"He will too! He will if you handle him right," Newt Jackson shrilled. "Let me get up there and drive and we'll make it."

Mama looked him up and down speculatively. "You'd add sixty pounds to the load if you swapped seats with either one of us. And we'd lose our coasting and have to get it started again."

He subsided in rage, began his fast trot around again.

"What you *could* do," she added mildly, "is ride behind or in front. Quit agitating him."

He glowered but swung ahead. The parade moved a foot forward.

"Oh Lord," said Mattilda in a loud voice, "thou knowest I never willfully hurt an animal in my whole life."

Beside her, Joe snorted with a sudden laugh. "Yea, Lord, thou knowest," he agreed.

"I never killed a chicken, no matter how much Mama pleaded with me to do it," Mattilda went on. "I never killed a lizard or a snake, not even a copperhead, and when one crossed my path, I gave him the right of way." She glanced up at her mother and Elizabeth and saw that their hands covered their smiles. Just so they didn't get her to giggling. "But now, Lord, this animal's time has come, and it would be merciful to let it go into eternal rest."

"Praying ain't fair," Newt Jackson roared, hunching so far around in his saddle he seemed almost hind part forward.

"Why not?" Mama asked pleasantly. "Nothing in the bargain about praying. You can pray if *you* want to."

"It would be merciful if thou wouldst help this horse die here and now," Mattilda went on, glib as a revival preacher.

"No, sir, it wouldn't, Lord," Newt scolded the sky, "That horse hadn't ought to be murdered thataway."

"Besides, it would wipe out a bad bargain when a neighbor took unfair advantage of us in our distress," Mattilda said silkily.

Newt Jackson swore, apologized to God, prayed on.

And yet, while the long prayer-argument continued, interspersed with snickers from Elizabeth and cheers from Joe in form of "Thou knowest" and "Yea, verily," Mattilda's mind went wide from the mark and she was split in her thought. She watched the valiant efforts the horse made and felt her own

138

shoulder all but heave toward him to help. *Live!* her mind commanded him. *Live!*

For she had long ago given up the land in her heart, and the prayer became a hypocritical whip to nip neat bits of flesh from Newt Jackson and not to entice the Lord into killing the horse.

I'll make it up to you if you'll try hard to live, she silently told the quivering animal.

"Lord, this poor horse is dying," she began again. (*I don't mean it, Lord.*) "It's a question of whether thou will grant thy mercy *now* or whether . . ."

"No, Lord," Newt moaned. "Dost thou intend to murder this beast on the word of this little witch?"

"Witch?" Mattilda hollered.

But the horse made it home, and Mattilda was there in a flash, unhitching it and rubbing away the sweat and comforting it with water. While she tended it, Newt Jackson laughed and boasted. "You done got prayed into the ground, Mattilda. You took on an *expert* this time." He left, still laughing, and on down the road his guffaws punctuated the air, but he was no more nuisance to her than a butterfly.

When Mattilda at last looked up from her work, she saw Joe standing between Mama and Elizabeth, his arms around their shoulders for support. His aged thin face watched her soberly. In the silence her heart stopped. His right leg was gone, and his pant leg was neatly folded and pinned against his thigh.

She ran to Joe, held him close, felt his head lean to touch her own. "Brother. Brother Joe. Oh, thank God you're home."

Forty-four

Mattilda spent all her spare time in the next three days rambling through the woods looking for proper limbs to be made into crutches. She would do anything to turn Joe into himself again, to erase the agonized stare from his face. The first thing was to get him independent. On his feet. Foot, her mind corrected. He had suffered too much. He had absorbed another shock when he tried to converse with Papa and had taken on a stricken look, as if his own soul were shriveling the way his father's had.

Now Mattilda cried in outrage, "The *idea* of the army sending you home without crutches!"

"Oh well," Joe said with indifference. "They would have given me crutches. If I'd be willing to wait."

"How long?"

He shrugged. "They had one pair the right size for a child. And that was all they had. Nobody worried about it much because the big problem was what we were going to find to eat for supper. If anything."

Mattilda had fetched a great pile of limbs for Joe to consider and still he couldn't decide where to start. He was skittish, she finally realized. Couldn't decide *anything* as long as she was there. The pressure of another person's presence was too much. Still too tender and sore. Still strung tight against sudden death.

"I'm going on in," she told him, "and when you pick one out, holler and I'll come hand it to you."

His eyes glazed with fear. Of what? she wondered. Being alone? Making the decision?

But he nodded and looked at the pile of sticks. She went inside the house, resolving to keep a close watch.

For a long time Joe sat shivering in the thin sunlight, his eyes glancing at the limbs and away, while Mattilda watched from the shadow of the window blind. Finally he seemed to settle on a choice, turned to call her, decided against it, braced himself against the bench with both arms and reached with his foot to disentangle a stick, used it to fork out the one he wanted. Looked at it. Hefted it for balance. Measured it from armpit to hand where a sloping branch would serve as a grip.

Finally took out his knife and began to whittle. She sighed and turned to her work, thinking that there was enough for her to do, God knew, without her hanging over Joe like a mother hen. She needed to be about her own business of learning to cook, an art she had neglected in her years of stubbornly working outdoors at men's work. What would Daniel think of her as he discovered the whole truth of the matter—that she knew almost nothing about keeping house? Now she struggled with cornmeal pudding, "easiest thing on earth to make," her mother had told her.

She glanced out. Joe stood upright, one hand clutching a stick for balance, the other arm snugged against his new crutch. He began a slow awkward walk around the yard, and she needed to blink away sudden tears, while "Maryland, My Maryland" swelled up with martial eloquence in her mind. She went outside and applauded. Joe's grin was still raw with pain.

"Soon as I get this thing sanded smooth, I'm going to whittle me a new leg."

She hadn't even thought of this. She studied Joe a moment, wondering that his terrible wound had not touched him deeper.

141

"Joe, did Grandpa Hume ever talk to you about dwindling?"

"Dwindling?" he laughed. "No, not that I remember. What was he talking about?"

She didn't try to explain. "Oh, nothing much. Didn't amount to anything."

Still she couldn't help marvelling that Joe had a natural ability to fight dwindling, and she had had to be taught.

Forty-five

December 1864

Christmas Eve day cleared up for a while and Mattilda rode Mac, their good brown horse, down the muddy road to the mill. It had become her daily vigil to look for a letter from Sarah. The letter never came. Often though, a letter from Daniel would give her trip home new interest and value and riding alone was pleasurable because she could read his letters over and over to her own satisfaction and then be able to pass on the news when she got home.

"Morning, Mattilda," Newt Jackson greeted her. "Going to lead prayer meeting this week?" Broad winks to the men working on the porch. Cessation of movement and grins all around. The story of their contest in prayers had gone the length of New Place Road, but it bothered her not at all.

"No, I'll leave it to the experts like yourself," she said. "I do believe that if you prayed as hard as you did to get our land, you could pray the War to a halt."

"*My* land," he corrected. She smiled. Newt Jackson was now the biggest landowner on the road and still he lacked her own quiet assurance. It was as if the land was hers forever, no matter who held the deed. Nobody could take away her growing up there, and nobody could put the feeling of ownership into Newt's head.

"You reckon I *could* pray the War to a halt?" he asked her.

"Don't doubt it in the least. It's your *duty* to," she assured him.

"I'll do it," he said fervently. "I'll pray the Confederates beat hell out of them, excuse me, and send them packing off home and this whole land be called Confederate States of America."

"Oh, good idea," she said. "Better do it in church."

In a happy daze from considering his new power, he said, "You got one from Bill and one from Daniel Durham telling about the saltworks being tore up."

"Saltworks?" The last she'd heard from Daniel, the Yankees were bypassing the saltworks and going on to Wytheville and the lead mines, and Breckenridge was sending out defenders on the train to Marion to meet Stoneman's Yankees. "We're getting into it again," Daniel had written, "and you'll think I'm silly but it's so cold and wet and miserable and boring that we look forward to *doing* something."

"Saltworks?" she repeated, disbelieving.

"Oh, Lord, yes," Newt said. "Y'all ain't heard about it? old General Stoneman took Bristol, took Abingdon, went to Wytheville, and our side stepped out to meet them, and beat them too. Then Stoneman sent a force to the saltworks and tore it up, burned and pillaged. Ran water into the salt that was near ready. Broke up the pumps and furnace. Tried to ruin the *kettles*." He laughed sharply. "Can you imagine? Those kettles will be there long after *they*'re gone."

"But in the meantime," Mattilda said, "where will the Confederacy get salt?"

"We stood in mud and rain at Marion for 38 hours," Daniel's letter read, "nothing to eat and no fire or shelter, and I heard not one soul to complain, though I had my complaining thoughts.

"I guess you know by now that they ruined the saltworks, apparently what they aimed to do all along, and we wasted our energy protecting the railroad. It cleared up Wednesday and we baked some weevily cornmeal cakes on the rocks in the sun, using water from the pits in the road. We had no salt, though we were near tons of it—if we could just get to it. The cakes tasted good anyway, not that I'd recommend them for every day.

"So never worry your head about your cooking. Whatever you cook will taste wonderful.

"Miss Repass, I'll tell you one thing you must *not* mention because it is only hearsay and I cannot tell it for the truth. We have heard that the defenders of the saltworks (not all, but *some* of them) were so angry that they killed all the wounded soldiers abandoned by the Federals. I have never heard of this happening before, not in a civilized war."

(*Civilized!*)

"To make it worse, these were the brave negro soldiers I told you about before, and they were pushed to the front by the Federals, wounded in a strong defense, then *slaughtered* by our side.

"My skin crawls with the thought of their treatment by *both* sides."

Mattilda shook her head in fury. It would be hard to keep quiet about it.

She turned to Bill's letter.

"My gun exploded in my hands." The words leaped up at

144

her out of the middle of Bill's letter. "It blew the fingers off my left hand except for the thumb and the first joint of the forefinger, I can still hold things but I'm clumsy at it."

She folded the letter and put it away, would read no more till she got home.

"Bill's hurt," she said, handing his letter to her mother.

Mama read the letter silently, the bitter lines down the sides of her mouth deepening. She finished the letter and stared at the log wall.

"This War has killed off a generation of our men," she finally said, choking with grief.

"Not killed, Mama," Mattilda said. "Bill's alive. So's Joe."

Her mother shrugged. "Killed or crippled. The cemetery is fuller than my house."

Mattilda was thankful Joe was at the barn because it wouldn't do for him to hear Mama now. Yet it seemed to her that every member of the family had been cruelly hurt. Papa. Mama because of her husband and children. Bland Junior killed. Sarah's Jason killed and Sarah with a boy to raise. Michael killed. Marjorie's Albert killed and Marjorie with a girl to raise. Beautiful Elizabeth too fearful to marry any of the young mountain soldiers, lest she be left to raise a child too. Joe and Bill so sorely wounded they'd be handicapped in farm work.

Everybody but herself.

Forty-six

March 1865

It was the kind of cold morning Mattilda loved for outdoor work, enjoying the feel of frozen twigs snapping underfoot and taking note of the slow thaw that would set in by midmorning. There would be early buds thrusting forth in determined announcement.

Strange now to be *inside* working at a furious rate to have dinner ready for her whole family when they came in from clearing. She worked with enthusiasm for it was a test. Could she cook a whole meal without help? "Of course you can. Don't be silly," her mother had said with some confused guilt because there were all those years she had not insisted on teaching her youngest daughter. But who would have done the farming if not Docia and Mattilda?

"Never mind," Daniel wrote her about her embarrassing ignorance. "You can broil it, bake it, grill it or leave it raw and it'll suit me. If worse comes to worst, *I* can cook over a fire though I'm not experienced with stove-cooking. We'll learn together. Don't forget, I have yet to set my hand to a plow and *you* will have to teach me." Oh, Daniel was good, so easy to confess to.

The house was redolent with the smell of fatback and shuck beans, onions sliced thin in grape vinegar, turnips simmering, smoky potatoes in the oven, and she had only the biscuit dough to mix and pat out in the great black pans at the last minute, but this was no problem because Mama had with careless competence thrown together the dry ingredients into the wooden bread bowl.

Mattilda relaxed long enough to check on Annie who slept in Marjorie's bed, fenced in by pillows, sucking her thumb noisily even in her sleep. She would awake in a rage of hunger before long, and Mattilda had the milk ready on the side of the stove. She stared with love down at the baby's pink face, clenched against waking as tight as her tiny fist. "God love your heart," Mattilda said passionately.

She heard the door open and reluctantly she left her niece to see who had come home for something forgotten. It was not time yet for dinner, and her family had barely begun to clear the new field of bramble and scrub, ready for planting, now that the rich cultivated fields belonged to the Jackson farm.

She was slow and comfortable in her thinking, completely unprepared for the shock of seeing Ray Beard, standing inside, leaning against the closed front door, insolently keeping his hat on.

A shimmering of goosebumps ran over her, as if she'd sluiced herself with ice water. It was a situation she didn't know how to handle.

"How do, Mattilda?" he said. Hat still on. No pretense of ordinary manners.

"Mama and Joe will be here in a minute," she said. "You got any business with us, you can take it up with them."

He shook his head, smiled at her, his eyes gleaming dully with a glint no sharper than that of a gun barrel. Dead eyes. Mattilda watched him, warily stayed a distance away, kept the table between them. Panic arose in her like an uncontrolled startle of birds.

"No, Mattilda. I just came by there, seen them working.

They'll not be here for two hours."

Her relief was immediate. "Oh, well then. They *will* be here if you came by there."

He continued to smile and to shake his head, his eyes now traveling greedily to her throat, her arms, her breast, her waist.

"Nope. I came by the creek."

It was all woods there. She and Docia had ridden it a hundred times, escaping the eyes of their families. Mattilda's breath came in uneven jerks as her fright built again. She chose her words carefully, afraid to enrage him, afraid she might start something. What? Something she couldn't stop?

"Mama wouldn't want you here. You go on now and see her later if you must. Go *on* now." Her voice cracked into a tiny shriek.

His smile left. "I came to see *you*, Mattilda, been wanting to know you better." He moved easily toward the table and started around. Mattilda moved fast to the other side, tried not to seem to be running. Her mind charged ahead at full speed. Thank God for her years of hard work and the strength she had developed. If it came to a fight, she would pitch in. Where was the kitchen knife? Too far. Too hard to get to without having him pounce. What other weapon? Nothing in reach. Gun loaded but lying full length in the pie safe under the linens. God, she thought. Now, God, I need help. Help me. Amen.

They circled the table twice, slowly, as if neither would admit a chase was taking place. She watched his dull eyes. No life in them. Oh, she thought with sudden surprise and accelerated terror, no *soul* in them. He was soulless. A man's body in pursuit of its wants, but soulless.

"You afraid of me, Mattilda?" he asked. "No need to be. I'm here *courting* you. This the way you treat Daniel Durham?"

His dead eyes held her.

148

"You don't get out now, I'm going to scream," she said, moving slowly around.

"You do that. I'd enjoy that. Not a soul to hear but me." Now he suddenly reversed and came around fast, she turning swiftly and keeping ahead.

But there *was* another soul to hear. Annie! Mattilda's fear built unbearably. Why, he would smash that baby without compunction, she believed, if she gave him half an excuse. She must try to lead him out of the house. On the next circle around the table she ran for the door, had it half open when he was on her, slamming the door, his right arm holding her with bruising strength, his left hand violently going over her body, cupping her breasts and squeezing. He whistled softly. "You are all there, Mattilda."

She felt filthy. She fought silently, must not scream and wake Annie. His hand touched her throat and face and she grabbed it and bit, felt *bone* between her teeth, tasted salty blood. Spat.

He howled, lifted her into the air, slammed her against the floor, leaned and hit her face with closed fist.

"Damn bitch," he said in fury. "You won't act right. I won't neither." His fist crunched against her jaw and she felt it sag loose.

Mattilda's senses left her briefly but almost immediately she recommenced her struggles, rolled away from him under the table, tried to get up to run.

He had her again, this time ripping her dress away, tearing her underclothes apart. He leaned against her.

"No. No. Don't do this, Ray Beard. Please. I'm not yet sixteen. Don't do this." She twisted and turned away.

He hit her again, took his pants down. "You plenty old to enjoy this. You wait now. It'll feel good in a minute."

She got almost up before he slammed her down again. He

149

twisted her head toward him. "Now you *look* at me."

Don't see, she commanded herself. Don't hear. Don't feel. Don't be a part of this horror.

But there was no escaping the pain that surged up inside her as he took her with savage force, and her screams began and continued without letup. He ignored the screams, hastened to completion, lay back with his eyes closed. She turned away, still screaming, hurting, bleeding. Sick. A man without a soul had stolen her own spirit and left her abraded and valueless. Her screams became sobs.

He looked up at her, his eyes not so dead now. There was blood where she had lain and he smiled. "I got to you first then." He thrust with his chin, through with her. For now. He got up, looked around as if he were in his own kitchen.

"I'll have some coffee and you can straighten things up a little. All right? You don't want them to know what happened, do you? Wouldn't do to tell Daniel Durham I got there first. Your mother would want us to get married right away, you know, and I wouldn't mind that myself, but I would want to come courting and do it right. You oughtn't of talked me into doing this."

Mattilda's amazement equalled her horror at his talk. In a minute she would start vomiting and would get rid of the ugly queasy feeling.

"I didn't tell you any such thing," she said, weeping bitterly.

"Who's going to believe that? Who won't believe me if I tell them we planned to meet here alone this morning? And that you teased me beyond my endurance? Be better to clean up and forget it. Not embarrassing to you that way."

The words went on and on, explaining, cajoling, commanding, and her confusion grew. Was it *true* that he was the first so she belonged to him? Was it true that her family and Daniel would believe it was *her* fault, that she had asked for it? Was it true that she had dirtied herself, that she had done this damage to herself? She shook with hate and pain. One thing she knew for certain: Ray Beard wasn't through with her yet.

"Damn baby howling," he said. She realized that Annie had been crying for a long time. Dazed but obedient to the summons, she wrapped herself up in her torn clothes as well as she could, started to the bedroom to see about the baby. Hurry! Annie may come creeping in.

"Wait!" he commanded.

She turned fearfully, tried to read his look. The eyes were going dead again.

She stood, still and tense, fighting renewed panic. "She just wants changing," she said, the words mumbled strangely. Her jaw must be broken.

"Let her be," he said, starting to get up.

"No. Let me change her," she pleaded. "That way we'd not be interrupted." She dropped her dress and petticoat, stood before him, naked except for the torn chemise. Heart pounding painfully.

"Oh ho. It's like I told you, is it?" He laughed, gave a wave that granted permission.

She flung open both doors of the pie safe, praying the gun wouldn't show, fumbled with the linens.

"What you doing?" he asked.

"Looking for a didy."

She had it, still hidden under the linens. She had never shot this gun but had spent one October learning to shoot with Papa as her teacher. Where was the trigger? There. She had it.

"What you *doing?*" he repeated loudly.

"Getting this didy," she said, turning and standing upright, swinging the gun around, finger ready on the trigger.

She watched her enemy. Took pleasure in his hissing gasp

and the quick sweat on his face, was entertained at the pale spindly legs, was full of hate for his whole being, was infuriated at his quick return of confidence when she didn't shoot.

"Now, Mattilda, you don't want no more today, it's all right. Whenever you want me, just let me know. But not today, all right?"

He moved with elaborate caution toward his clothes.

"Don't move another step." she said. "We'll wait till my folks come . . ."

He froze in a crouch. Presently moved again, straightening himself.

"You want them to see us like this? You going to let them know what you done?"

Confusion. Uncertainty. The gun barrel described a small wavering circle. The triumphant look in his eyes alerted her to his action. She barely had time to aim and shoot as he sprang.

The roar was stupefying and she fell backward from the gun's kick, coughed through the rolling smoke, grasped the gun firmly and swung it back like a club.

No need. Ray Beard sat on the floor looking with wild concern at the gaping hole in his crotch. His hands frantically tried to hold his slithering innards in place. Failed. He grabbed and tucked, grabbed again, looked up at her in horror. The swift slippery blood made his task harder.

She held the gun at parade rest as she had watched Bill and her father do at militia drill.

"No, Ray Beard," she said. "Not today. Nor tomorrow either."

She waited and watched. Mama and Joe would be on their way by now. Gunshot sounds carry.

Ray Beard kept trying. He was too busy to listen to her.

"You remember Jason?" she asked conversationally. No

answer. Only a frantic tucking in and holding, then grabbing again. "Jason should be here. First, there was Jason. And there was Sarah. And then there was me." She paused. "And now there's you."

Ray Beard's hands suddenly relaxed in his lap and were immediately full, all his work gone for naught. His head leaned to the side against the chair, and his eyes stared ceilingward, more sharply alive than they had been when they could see.

Mattilda waited. He was dead all right. She got a quilt and wrapped herself in it, went to tend Annie, the second time she'd taken care of her dressed in this quilt.

Her rage and loathing did not lessen as she fed Annie, as she heard her mother scream "My God, it's Ray Beard's horse," as she heard the door flung open and heard Joe's crutch thud on the floor, as she heard them talk in quick, soft phrases, as she nodded to the question "Did he get you?" as she received the reassurance of her mother's arms.

All those things were remote and unreal, and she knew she would never be rid of the only realities—the hate and the fury.

Forty-seven

While her mother bathed Mattilda and dressed her, talking in a soft familiar baby talk (calling her Peejib, that long-ago baby name), the rest of the family got Ray Beard into the wagon, flung dusty grain sacks over him. Her whole family rode guard, guarding *her*, not Ray Beard, Mattilda knew. They went to Judge Stinson's office for an immediate hearing. Mattilda had quit shaking, had become still as death, but with only her mama in the office with her and the judge, she got through the story, told him the way it had happened, knowing she could trust him to keep silent about the rape. Sometimes he had to ask her a question two or three times to draw her out of her dream.

Her mind fastened to the dream. She was fishing under the bluff with Sarah and they were not talking or moving much, just enjoying the sun and being together.

After each answer Judge Stinson drew from her, she returned to the dream.

Finally the judge said with distaste, "Tell them to leave Beard inside the hall, and I'll have him picked up." He kept Mattilda and her mother inside with him till the body was out of sight. "No need of further hearing, Miss Mattie," he told her. "It was a justified act of defense." He shook hands with her and Mama.

On the way home, Mattilda stayed in the dream. Once Sarah caught a fish, flipping silver in the sun in happy abandon, it seemed, and without pain.

Forty-eight

Two Mattildas walked in one body, one following the old routines of farming, sewing, cooking, talking to her family. But the second Mattilda, strange and secret, was in firm control, looking in sudden fear behind her when she went to the mill, listening with silent hatred to the arrogant masculine gossip, which had never disturbed her before. Remembering the gun blast. Wishing that she would awake soon and be through with this nightmare. The secret Mattilda put aside her mother's anxious looks, her sisters' efforts to talk, Joe's little gifts of love. Lay all this aside, the secret Mattilda whispered, because it's not real, and if you believe in it, it will *touch* you and arouse your dead soul. You'll hurt again.

The kitchen floor was scrubbed to a decent white, but often the secret Mattilda plainly saw the spots of blood she had lost there, and then to overcome the shaking terror, she swung her gaze a little and watched Ray Beard grappling with nervous haste.

Her whole family was in the kitchen, busy with evening activities: Mama darning socks on her beautiful darning ball Joe had whittled, Joe on his cot shaping up a violin he swore he would make, if it took the rest of his life, Marjorie and Annie in the rocker (madonna and child), Elizabeth popping corn.

Mattilda and Papa sat at the table, silent and apart, taking no part in the conversation, despite all the attempts the family made to draw them in.

Mama put her darning down and came to sit with them, took Mattilda's hand while the secret Mattilda braced and stiffened. She spoke quietly, "Mattie, it's not fair to quit writing to Daniel. He knows you had to kill Ray Beard. He would want you even if he knew—uh—the rest, what you went through. Don't you believe that?"

The hidden Mattilda exposed herself with sudden vicious anger, "But I don't want Daniel." Immediately the old Mattilda regretted the stunned look on her mother's face.

I know, Mama, she thought. You're worried that I haven't had my period. You're afraid for me, for what will become of me if I'm pregnant. Don't you mind. I'll never in this world give birth to Ray Beard's child. First, I'll die, and then *it* will die, poor innocent monster.

"Then you must tell Daniel and turn him free," her mother said.

So Mattilda got a sheet of paper and wrote, "Dear Mr. Durham, I now find I no longer wish to continue our friendship. Mattilda Repass." She handed the letter to her mother, said good night to her family, went to bed, her eyes taking swift care to see that every window blind was safely closed.

Forty-nine

April 1865

Daniel Durham came with a rented buggy, spending all his money in this effort to win Mattilda back, she felt sure, as well as being away from his company without leave. Her mother's whispered insistence was strong. "You go with him and explain. You owe him that much."

So she climbed into the buggy, shying away from his extended hand, sat far to the right and stared at the woods, noting solemnly that the soft touches of pale spring green failed to move her. They were quiet, but once their glances touched, Daniel's blue eyes baffled and sick. Blue-eyed Scot, she thought without affection.

"The Federals finished off the railroad plumb to Lynchburg," he said. "We can't stop them. I think the War is nearly over." He looked at her, hoping she would take up the conversation, but her secret self resisted him and steered her away from her curious feeling of hope.

"I'll be home for good soon, I think," he said. "Though nobody will admit it, our army is dying on its feet." He waited. She kept her silence.

"I'll be home for good and I want to be with you more," he said.

She shook her head. "It's all different now, Daniel. Things won't ever be as they were."

He rushed swiftly in, to keep the conversation afloat. "Why, Mattilda? Why should it matter to *us*? You should feel no guilt about killing him. You had a right to protect yourself. Why will it be different?"

She told him, using the ugly word that *nobody* used.

"He raped me."

Utter confusion, then massive heaving of shoulders and sobs. Daniel crying! For a moment the old Mattilda wanted to reach out a comforting hand, bur the new bitter Mattilda thought, Um hm, crying over that all-important thing I've lost. Crying because *you* didn't get there first.

"Why are you crying, Daniel?" she asked roughly.

He looked up, amazed that she would ask. "I'm crying because he hurt my baby. I'm crying that you killed him, that I didn't get to do it. I'm crying because *I want to kill him*."

Ah, she knew how he felt. Sometimes when she relived her nightmare, she wished passionately that Ray Beard had lived longer, that she had smashed his face with the gun, that she had kicked him, that she had worked out her hate on him.

But Daniel had called her his baby. Did he think of her that way? The two Mattildas momentarily slipped into one person, and she softened toward Daniel.

"There's one more thing, Daniel. I've not had my period."

"Oh." He reached for her hand, didn't insist when she kept away. "Then we should get married right now."

"No, I'll not give birth to a monster."

"Monster?" he said without understanding. "*Your* baby?"

157

"I'll never have it," she said. "And you mustn't come again until I know for sure. It's my pain to work out and you can't help."

He took her home, unable to persuade her. They shook hands in formal farewell, and while Mattilda felt no grief at his leaving, she felt better, still patchy as a quilt but at least together.

Fifty

Her separateness continued. Her family's efforts to reach her intensified.

"What did Daniel say?" Mama asked. "Or rather, what did *you* say?"

It took courage for her mother to ask, Mattilda knew, for a week had passed without her saying a word about her conversation with Daniel. Her mother had the apologetic look people get when they said, "None of my business, but I was wondering . . ."

"Oh, nothing much," Mattilda replied, trying to look as if she were telling the whole truth. "I told him what happened."

Mama waited. "And that's *all?*"

"Well, I told him I might be pregnant."

Her mother's eye pupils enlarged, giving her a sharp attentive look. "And *that's* all? You might *not* be pregnant too. Sometimes *fear* of being pregnant will stop the periods. But what did Daniel have to say to that?"

Mattilda could go no further without confessing that Daniel had renewed his proposal, which would invite immediate urgings from her mother. So she turned away and went obstinate. Nothing would make her agree to marry Daniel and have Ray Beard's baby.

Bill and Joe began building another room and Mattilda's thoughts dwelt on their angry stumps, fingers and leg, and on her own hurt. How could they go on the way they did? Never admitting to the fact that part of them had died.

The exhilaration of the two young men at being home, brother with brother, burst out in laughter and song, and Mattilda sat at the window, the stillness within her untouched by their noisy joy except by a mild astonishment that their wounds had been only surface.

"Hey, Mattie, come help us," Joe called every so often.

She never answered. Let them play the fool all they wanted—she would take no part.

"Hey, Mattie," Joe called again. "You got company." She felt a brief panic but refused to answer. It would be Daniel, and she'd not see him.

She waited, tense and afraid, heard a slow stumbling movement into the house, heard Bill saying, "There now, you made it." Turned to look, couldn't believe it was Grandpa Hume, first time she'd seen him since he had moved back home.

He was old, old, swaying in the door uncertainly, trembling, holding a nervous hand to the doorframe for steadiness. Trying to adjust his vision to see her in the darkened room. To *think* that he had made this struggle for her.

"Mattie, honey?" His voice had gotten small.

Emotion flowed in her like water, and she couldn't resist him though she was angry at whoever fetched him up. It was no fair way to act. It was taking advantage of her love for the

159

old man. She rose to meet him, and they held each other without words.

"Now tell me how it is, Mattie," he directed her. They sat together in the sitting part of the big room, which was suddenly vacated by the family. She tried to think what to say. Hard to explain to him what she wasn't sure of herself.

"Well," she ventured. "You know Bill and Joe were wounded."

He nodded, watched her closely, didn't try to make it easy for her. She tried to accustom herself to his sagging face, the worn look, the trembling right arm. Tried to return to the easy comfort she used to have with him. How could he possibly hope to give her strength? There was not the slightest doubt in her mind that this was his reason for coming.

"It's like I'm wounded too," she said.

He nodded. "I can understand that. I'm wounded myself. Look at this." He held up his arm, watched it flap like a starling's wing. Laughed. "That's *my* wound. I can't hold the damn thing still."

Her depression deepened. Everybody was sick or sore or hurt, even Grandpa Hume, and he *laughed* about it. He surely could not understand.

"It's the scar of my war wound," he said, grinning at his palsied arm. "Just like your war wound."

"How you mean—*war* wound?"

"Strain. Harder work than I could do. Fear of the War and what it was doing to us. And so on. Likely my wound would have come anyway but later on and not so bad. Like *your* war wound. Attacked by a man whose natural viciousness was brought out by the War. Without the War you'd never been left alone while the rest of the family was out on the farm."

It was true. These were war wounds. But what difference did it make? The shriveling went on in her spirit as if she were

160

a tree being fiercely denuded by caterpillars. She could all but hear the crunching jaws eating her soul. And she didn't care whether or how soon she would vanish completely.

"And you aren't dwindling?" she asked.

His laughter was quick. "Dwindling? Hell, no, honey." He clapped his shaking arm. "That ain't *me*. That's only my arm. I pet it and care for it all I can, stroke it and say, 'There now, old arm,' but it still ain't *me*. No indeed."

"I might be pregnant," she said, to show him the hopelessness of her own wound.

He studied her face. "You're ashamed to have a baby, thinking people will say, 'There goes Mattilda Repass carrying Ray Beard's baby'."

It was too savage a question and she winced.

"Yes, ashamed. Yes, angry. Yes, afraid. I'll not *have* his child."

He waited till she calmed. "You're telling me now that you'll kill yourself, and this scares me, honey. You're telling me good-bye, is that it? You're telling me to get ready for an empty world." His tears suddenly flowed and he took her in his arms, held her close, his good hand pressing her head into his shoulder, and they wept together.

"What else can I do?" she cried. "How can I *live?*"

Grandpa Hume quieted and began talking slowly. "Your wound will heal, given time, like any other wound. But right now you got to hew *against* the grain. Take your worries one at a time and *live* them. Say you want to cut away your worry about Ray Beard. It's easy to try to forget it, but don't do that. *Live* it. Let it hurt. Then holler, cry, rage, cuss!"

Grandpa Hume telling her to *cuss?*

"That's hacking across tough wood, a little cut at a time. That's lopping out the useless part with a broadaxe."

His good left arm chopped the air.

161

"Then get into your work again, even if you feel you're only going through motions. Watch for a chance to look at a tree or listen to a bird. Go easy and slow. That's how I cured *my* wound."

She had never in her whole life known Grandpa Hume to be wrong.

"All right, I'll try," she promised.

But inside, her selfness huddled in an enamelled, rejecting ball, unmoving and untouched.

Fifty-one

The boys were at the milldam, fishing for supper, when the word came, so Mattilda and Marjorie saddled up and rode down to tell them. Newt Jackson was quiet for once, his face secretive.

"Did you *hear,* Newt?" Marjorie shouted.

He put a finger to his lips and his eyes rolled wildly. "Shhh. Shhh. Hush."

He ran down the mill steps to them, talked low so that the people on the porch and those in an approaching wagon wouldn't hear. "We don't want the word to get around. *Lee* surrendered. *They* surrendered, out yonder. *We* ain't surrendered and don't intend to. We're going to whip them yet."

Mattilda and Marjorie looked at each other in bewilderment, and Marjorie burst out laughing.

Mattilda turned to the people in the wagon, a woman and two half-grown boys. "The War is over," she said. "Lee surrendered to Grant. The War is over."

The woman lifted her hands up to the side of her head like rabbit ears and her mouth opened in amazement. "Praise the Lord," she said. She reached to hug her sons, then wheeled the wagon in a circle and went back home.

"See what you done?" Newt growled.

Joe struggled up the path, and Bill burst through the woods, reached his good hand to Joe to help him past a bad place.

"The War's over, brothers," Mattilda said. She waited for them to have a joyful reaction as her sisters and mother had had, but their faces were blank and still.

"What happened?" Joe asked.

"General Lee surrendered yesterday to General Grant. It's all over."

Her brothers' faces were pale.

"Thank you," Joe said. They turned back to the creek in silence and the two women started home.

It was strange, Mattilda thought. The War was over, and her side had lost. She had regarded it as joyful because the other women in her family had, but they had not thought of the effect it would have on her brothers.

She felt no joy herself. She had lost the War when Ray Beard entered the door.

How soon, she wondered, would morning sickness begin? When it did, there would be no doubt, and she would find a way to escape her family for a while. It didn't need to be long.

Fifty-two

The War was over, but occasional bands of marauders, Federal and Confederate renegades, still robbed the countryside of stock and grain, so every morning someone must drive the cow through the woods to a hidden pasture and go in the evening to fetch her home.

Mattilda wished she might go by herself, felt safer in the woods than at home, wanted time for her thoughts to drift as they pleased without the interruption or pressure of another person.

But Mama panted beside her, full of distrust, fearful that Mattilda would climb the cliff and leap. Oh, she knew her mother's mind. It worked alongside her own mind as parallel as railroad tracks, with both of them pretending to be thinking other things and each mind checking the other with thoughts as soft as snail feelers.

Her mother kept a steady flow of complaint to Gentle, the cow, directing her. In other times, Mattilda would have been reduced to giggles, knowing how easy it was to persuade Gentle down the path, with only a touch of the switch, never a need to hit or scold.

They worked her down to the road toward the pasture path, and as always, looked up and down the road for the sight of travelers. The road was empty both ways, mill and church, and they started into the woods, Gentle leading.

Mattilda thought she had glimpsed a horse, stepped back into the road to look, for riders coming from the mill often stopped at their house to give the news.

"Think I see somebody, Mama. Hold up, Gentle." She laid a hand on the cow's neck. Together they waited for the rider to appear again around the hill.

"Slow as seven-year itch if it *was* somebody," her mother said.

There it was, a horse (mule?) being led by someone. "It's a woman," they said together, quirking their mouths sideways in acknowledgement of their minds working in tandem.

They waited patiently. Likely someone needing help was heading for Mama's knowledge and store of herbs.

The woman's face was shadowed by her sunbonnet.

"Who in the world?" Mattilda said. "Seems like I know her."

"She walks just like Grandma Justice," her mother announced.

"Somebody riding, a littl'un," Mattilda said.

"It couldn't be . . ." her mother said, her voice low. "It *couldn't* be? . . .

At this moment the woman looked up, pushed her bonnet back and stared. She tried to hurry the stolid mule along.

"Sarah!" Mama screamed. "Sarah! Sarah!"

She and Mattilda were off and running, leaving Gentle in consternation for only a moment before she went obediently down the path through the woods.

It *was* Sarah. Her free hand waved and waved. And there she came, stringy and lean where she had been slender, not so straight any more, her mouth taut and grim, a permanent crease between her brows. She wore an anxious look she never used to have. And still it was Sarah, loving and beloved.

Mother and daughter rushed together, clung, and Mattilda's

eyes blurred as she remembered the last time when Sarah had cried out, "Mama, what's *happening* to us?"

And now it was her turn to be hugged with a fierce hunger she had not known Sarah felt.

"I heard you killed him, and I came home to thank you for it," Sarah said. "It was justice."

She could not know about the rape, kept tight secret in the family. Never mind now, Sarah was home, her whole family was home (not Michael, not Bland Junior, a wispy thought reminded). But what was left of her family was together again.

And hearing Sarah thank her turned loose the hidden ball of rejecting self till it began to flow within her to all of her body and become part of her again. She relaxed and began to cry.

"My gracious, I haven't even met my grandson," her mother said. All three women turned toward the little boy who sat the mule like a man. His brown eyes surveyed them solemnly.

"He's the spitting image of his daddy," Mama said.

Sarah nodded and smiled. "Acts like him. Walks like him."

"My daddy died in the War," he announced to Mattilda.

"I know," she agreed, adult to adult.

"Was you in the War?" he asked.

"I sure was," she said fervently.

"Whose side was you on?"

It was awkward. Sarah was still new and strange—they had not completely returned to each other. But she must answer honestly.

"I don't know. When your daddy died, I was on the North's side. When Michael died, I leaned to the South. When southern soldiers stole food from Bland Countians, I hated them, but when the North burned our house, I hated *them*. And when I talk to Docia, I'm always on your daddy's side."

166

She took a deep shaky breath. "And when *I* was wounded, I hated the whole War and everybody in it. So I just don't know. I don't reckon I'm on anybody's side."

Jason, already through with the question and bored with the answer, kicked at the mule. "Come on, Mulehead, let's go."

Mattilda laughed. "Mulehead?" Sarah would be amazed to discover that *old* Mulehead was still alive, an expensive and sentimental luxury for all the good he was to them.

They started toward home, young Jason walking now and clutching Mattilda's hand as if he'd always known her. She was silent, listening to the eager talk between her mother and sister.

Suddenly she felt a twisting pain low in her bowels. It panged again.

"Mama," she said, keeping her voice even against her sudden hope, "it feels like I'm starting my period."

Her mother's face lighted, and Sarah looked up questioningly.

"Go on home and check," her mother urged. Mattilda ran like a race horse.

"Don't run," her mother called. Mattilda knew what *that* meant. In case you're pregnant after all. She ran on.

Her nervousness would hardly let her latch the privy door. Hurry, hurry. She inspected her britches. There it was. It was the first time in her life she was thankful to see blood.

She burst forth from the privy and headed for the house.

"I've got it! I've got it!" she screamed joyfully, while Sarah and Mama laughed.

Joe and Bill poked their heads out in puzzlement.

"Got what?" Joe said.

"I fell off the roof," Mattilda shouted.

"Mat-TIL-da," her mother scolded, still laughing.

"My God, are you hurt?" Joe said, limping out. He

realized what she was saying, turned red, grinned. "Oh. I'm sure glad."

"What?" Bill said. "What?" Joe turned to explain. Then they saw Sarah and hurried to her, but Mattilda ignored them all and started turning expert wagonwheels across the yard, her skirt and feet flying while behind her Jason rolled on the grass and squealed, and Mama shouted, "Now, Mattilda Repass, you stop that. You hear me? You stop that."

But on they whirled, aunt and nephew, feckless and foolish as kittens, till at last they tumbled together in helpless laughter and exhaustion.

Fifty-three

June 1865

Mattilda had changed again, almost to her true self. The dwindling had ceased. She and Docia sat in the swing, keeping it in motion with their toes.

Docia's eyes were knowing. "Ray Beard attacked you, didn't he?" Attack equals rape.

"Yes." No sense denying what Docia's quick mind had thought out of hiding.

"But you ain't expecting." Certainty in her voice.

"No. But I *thought* I was."

"I knew it."

"How could you tell?"

"You been distracted out of your mind, didn't hear me when I asked you something, quit talking, even about Daniel.

Talked about dying a few times. I knew how you felt." Docia gave her a strange, angry look.

"It happened to me once too."

Mattilda was stunned. "When? Who?"

"The night Lucas came home to die."

"Oh *no*. Who did it?"

Docia's anger was hot and lively as lava. "Your Uncle George."

Mattilda was aghast, sick. "Well, did you tell Mama? Or Papa?"

"No. 'It's a nigger's place to accommodate and keep shut about it,' he explained to me." Her words snapped like twigs.

"Well, *damn* his soul," Mattilda said. "Forever. Amen."

"Don't say that, not even about him," Docia said, her voice low.

They were quiet with their rage. Finally Mattilda added, "We can be thankful we weren't pregnant."

"I was. Mama helped me pass it," Docia said.

"Oh," Mattilda remembered now—Docia's long silence and half-sickness following Lucas's death.

"I wish you'd told me."

"I almost did. But Lucas just got killed by whites, and a white man did that to me, *your* uncle, and for a while I had trouble separating you from other white people."

"I know, I can see that." Mattilda wished bitterly that things had been different.

"When I get married, . . ." She stopped, hesitated. It was the first time she'd said that in a long time. "When I get married, we're going to build an extra room as soon as we can, and you'll come visit me so we can talk all we want, no one to tell us no, and we'll fix the meals together and explore the woods."

"And tend the babies," Docia said slyly.

"Well. Yes." Mattilda had to laugh at the way Docia punctured her balloons. "Never mind. You *will* visit me and we'll just be ourselves."

"All right, I will. If you'll visit *me*."

"Well, certainly, I will."

They were silent again, moving the swing barely enough to make it squeak.

"Tell me, Docia, what does sajer mean?"

Docia snickered. "First you tell me what nigger means."

Mattilda pondered. There was a question about that?

"Nigger means a bad black person."

"A *bad* one? Then how come white people call *all* of us niggers?"

Mattilda felt guilty. She'd done it herself. "I don't know."

Docia considered. "A sajer is a white nigger."

"And *I'm* one?"

"No," Docia scoffed. "That's only when we were fighting. You been huffing about that all these years?"

Mattilda shook her head, knowing she was lying a little. The conversation faded comfortably.

"I disown him as an uncle," she suddenly said. "You wait and see. Next time he comes, I'll call him *George* and if he scolds me for it, I'll tell him I can't think of him as kinfolks any more, and if he goes on about it, I'll tell him why."

"Do it. I don't care."

They were reluctant to give up talking, but at last they arose, and Docia said, "I hate to say good night. Been so long since we've talked, and any time now you'll go your way and I'll go mine."

Sadness as compelling as music came over Mattilda, and when they said good night, the words caught in her throat.

Fifty-four

Mattilda went outside by herself before the wedding began. Now she understood Marjorie's agitation at *her* wedding when she spent the day at her loom.

It was a nippy November day, and the cold got through to her, trussed up though she was in corset and wedding suit and new gloves. She must go in to be with Papa now.

Long before the wedding, Mattilda had (and won) two arguments with her mother. She would *not* be married in the church, she said. Why should she? They had a perfectly good house.

"What kind of wedding we going to have in *this?*" her mother had asked her, helplessly swinging her hand in a half-circle.

"I'm not ashamed of this house," Mattilda had stormed. The argument ended there, and Mama began to plan seriously.

In the second argument Mattilda had insisted upon her father's giving her away. "You'll be sorry," her mother said. "You better have Joe instead. He'll get mixed up and embarrass you in front of Daniel's folks."

"Better than having him think suddenly, Why ain't *I* giving her away?" Mattilda retorted. "Besides I want my *papa* to give me away. What's so hard about saying *I do?* I'll tutor him for a week if you think I should."

And he was ready, she thought. Everybody was ready. She

171

gave her mountains a look. Good-bye, mountains. I've new mountains to learn.

Daniel's wagon stood ready too, already hitched to their two horses, and packed with all their goods: their clothes, bed covers, her hydrangea, her crock of dough starter, the pans her family could spare her plus the new skillet from Grandpa Hume, the Bible from her parents, two chairs, sacks of flour and salt, kegs of honey and molasses, axes, seeds, a crate of wondering, questioning chickens; oh a wealth of goods. "How will it all go into that little shack?" Daniel had wondered.

"Well, it's *surely* bigger than the wagon, isn't it?" she responded with a laugh.

He nodded, but his grin was doubtful.

She slipped into the girls' bedroom where her father waited for her. He clutched his map. Mercy, she was in for it.

He *never* let the map be in a different room. The day Sarah came home, she gave it to him. "Look at this, Papa. A map of your family's long trip to New Place. See? Here's the first New Place where your grandparents lived, next to Staunton, then the trail where they walked down to Kerrs' Creek north of Lexington and coming on down to Irish Settlement—"

"Wait! Wait! That's wrong," Papa said in great excitement. They came across the mountain right *here.*" He stabbed a finger down.

Sarah handed him a pencil she had ready. "All right, Papa, you fix it."

He immediately huddled over the outspread map, went to work.

"Why didn't I think of that?" Mama marvelled.

Now he held the map, ready to carry it to the ceremony. Well, let him.

In the big room Joe started the fiddle music, thin and sweet, and she peeked through the door crack. Her family was all there, her sisters and mother standing in a line, half-smiling, a likeness about them, a sadness she couldn't fathom. They surely must be glad *somebody* in the family would be married.

Docia and Luella stood near Grandpa Hume, the only one seated, and behind him was Bill. Daniel's mother stood alone on the groom's side of the altar. She took swift anxious looks at the bedroom doors.

The room was beautiful, a whole wall covered with the giant mums Mama had worked so hard to raise.

Would Papa really mess everything up?

Daniel and his father, both stooping at the door, came out of her parents' room. The music changed, became brisk. Mattilda took her father's arm; his other hand clutched his map. She decided she didn't *care* whether he messed things up, they would get through it somehow or other.

Her father hesitated, looked puzzled. He needed one arm for Mattilda, one for his cane.

"I'll take it, Papa." She took the map and carried it to her wedding. Her heart began pounding at such a furious rate she could barely see Daniel. Oh beautiful, that Daniel, blue eyes loving her.

"Who gives this woman?" They waited, tense.

Her father spoke in a clear strong voice. "God knows it hurts to give her. This is Mattilda, our baby daughter, who kept us brave throughout our time of adversity."

Mattilda waited, moved by what her papa said, but apprehensive that his speech would go on and on, become a harrangue about the War.

"Yet I do freely give her, because we have no right to keep her, and it is a good man I give her to."

She felt his arm tremble. He turned to her. "But it's hard, Mattie."

173

Mattilda fought back her tears. O little, thin, bald-headed Papa. He had never been so dear to her. How could she *think* of leaving him? She glanced around at her family, saw that other eyes glistened.

Her father eased his arm away, took her hand and placed it in Daniel's. At once she felt better. She moved close to Daniel, ready for her vows.

"Where's my map?" Papa suddenly asked.

"Oh. Here, Papa," Mattilda said, handing him the roll of paper. There was a comfortable sound of chuckles around the room.

She took a quick look about. I'll remember all of this, she promised herself. The wall of mums was magnificent. Thank you, Mama. Something else caught her eye. The kitchen table, pushed to the corner and covered with white linen, had a small blue bowl of bright red bittersweet on it. That would be Sarah's work.

Bittersweet was so right, Mattilda thought. She hugged Daniel's arm and listened to the words.